A SHINY
CHRISTMAS STAR

A SHINY CHRISTMAS STAR

An Old West Christmas Trilogy

Steven Douglas Glover

For Monti
You played an important part in
the realization of this book.
Friends always,

Steven Douglas Glover

iUniverse, Inc.
New York Lincoln Shanghai

A SHINY CHRISTMAS STAR
An Old West Christmas Trilogy

iUniverse books may be ordered through booksellers or by contacting:

iUniverse
2021 Pine Lake Road, Suite 100
Lincoln, NE 68512
www.iuniverse.com
1-800-Authors (1-800-288-4677)

This is a work of fiction. All of the characters, names, incidents, organizations and dialogue in this novel are either the products of the author's imagination or are used fictitiously.

ISBN-13: 978-0-595-40003-4 (pbk)
ISBN-13: 978-0-595-84390-9 (ebk)
ISBN-10: 0-595-40003-5 (pbk)
ISBN-10: 0-595-84390-5 (ebk)

Printed in the United States of America

Dedicated to the memory of

Mary Elizabeth Glover
1948–2003

and

Louis L'Amour
1908–1988

Very Special Recognition to Linda Glover, without whom this book would've
been just a dream within my heart.

Special thanks also to the following, my fan club,
for their encouragement and support.

Monti Eastin
Verna Glover
Sandy Sheppard
Debra Hesson
Brenda Taylor
Jean West
Mary Hughes
Betty Richardson
Diane Harada
Lois Weller

"A SHINY CHRISTMAS STAR"

It was only three days before Christmas and I woke that morn with a chill in my bones. I shivered somewhat. I had been dreaming fitfully all night about a darkened cabin somewhere in the wilds of the Colorado territory. It was like my senses were telling me that someone or something was in deep trouble and needing help.

I lay there in the small room that I occupied at the Sumner Horse Ranch with my eyes closed for a long while. Blurry details of the ominous dream kept seeping into my mind and I tried to recall all that had passed before my weary eyes. I recalled snow and lots of it. I saw small children huddled together and close to starving to death. I foresaw pestilence and death.

I gritted my teeth and squinted my eyes against the vision that nagged my mind, but I, for the life of me, could not shake it. Each time that I closed my eyes, I saw a very small person reaching out for my hand.

I couldn't sleep. The foreboding dream kept churning within my soul and wouldn't let go. I tried four or five times to turn in various directions in hope of sleep, but to no avail. Something was terribly amiss somewhere close by and being the U.S. Marshal for the lower Colorado Territory, it seemed that I was destined to solve it.

Finally, I couldn't take it any longer. I slipped out of my warm layer of blankets and when my bare feet touched that icy cold floor, I quickly drew a breath.

"Damn, it is really cold in here. It must be freezing out there." were my immediate thoughts.

I exhaled with a rush and if it had been lighter out I would have seen the frost of my breath. I hastily dressed my six foot lanky frame in rumpled dark trousers, dark blue wool winter shirt, and boots. Then, I quietly made my way down the short hallway to the fireplace pausing only a moment or so at Laura's door. It was slightly ajar and I took a quick peek in. She lay towards the wall and seemed to be sleeping soundly. I smiled a bit at the womanly fragrance of her room, then continued on to the living room and the fireplace. I found that there were some still smoldering coals from the previous night's warming fire. I took some tinder and tossed it lightly on the coals. New flames momentarily licked at the sparse fuel while I wrestled up a couple of good "winter" logs to the fireplace. A few moments later brought crackling warmth to the room.

It was at that very moment that "Lady", Laura's blonde haired dog, appeared beside me, sticking her cold nose up against my back. That movement caused a shiver to ripple straight up my spine.

"Doggone it, Lady, that's cold. I'll get you for that. Come on, I'll let you out."

I opened the door for her and she lowered her head and sniffed outside. She balked at going out the door and started to back up.

"Oh, no, you don't. You put that cold nose on me. Get yourself out in that cold."

Lady reluctantly slipped out the door and I had to laugh. I knew that she would be back within a few minutes. I once again turned my attention toward that fireplace. Within moments a flame burst and suddenly I felt the first warmth of the morning. I waited for a few long moments, savoring the initial warmth. I nodded my head slightly. Now, for some hot coffee.

Lady was pawing the door, so I let her back in. She had a most pitiful look on her face.

"A little bit cool out there, huh? All right, go climb back in bed with Laura."

I stepped quickly into the icy cold kitchen and immediately sought out the kindling. Within minutes, I had a good fire going in that old cast iron stove. I filled that old blue spatterware pot with cold water and set it on the stove. Then, grinding up a hand full of coffee beans, I tossed the grounds into the pot.

I sat down then at the small kitchen table and reached into my shirt pocket. I pulled out the makings, rolled myself a smoke and lit it with a sulfur match. I drew deeply on the tobacco and blew myself a smoke ring. It seemed a long ten minutes before the coffee was ready and the rich flavorful aroma filled the kitchen. I inhaled deeply of it. The smell of freshly brewed coffee was always my first pleasurable moment of the day. Finally, I poured myself a cup of that strong black coffee and sat back to ponder more about the nightmarish dream that robbed me of a good nights sleep.

Seconds later, Laura Sumner, my best friend and lady love, dressed only in her night clothes consisting of woolen gown, heavy robe, and wooly slippers stepped quickly into the kitchen. Her dark brown hair was all tousled and she fairly looked a fright. Lady was beside her, and nuzzling her cold nose against her leg.

I grinned inwardly to myself.

"Lord, Cole! It is really cold this morning. Pour me a cup of that coffee please. I have been shivering all night, and besides that, I had some awful dreams. There was something about **little people** and, dammit, Cole; I just don't know what it means. There was a great blanket of white and short, little people crying for help. I can't put it out of my mind."

Laura sometimes had premonitions or dreams that somewhat foretold of things to come and if she had dreamed similar to me, I couldn't just let that pass. I looked directly into Laura's crystal blue eyes and sort of cocked my head to one side, "You dreamed of this?"

"Yes Cole, I dreamed of what seemed to be a darkened cabin within a forest area. It was snowing hard and furious and there seemed to be small people huddled together shivering. I just don't know what it means."

"I don't know what to say, Laura. I dreamed something of the same sort. I don't know what it means either, but if you also dreamed it, then something is amiss. You ain't missed a spell of danger yet within your dreams and I for one am not going to dismiss it. Something is coming and it will be a trial to resolve."

Presently, a knock came at the door. I told Laura to sit and enjoy her coffee. I tramped out of the kitchen, across the wide living room and found Judd Ellison, Laura's Foreman, standing on the porch wrapped up in his heaviest winter coat, stomping his feet and rubbing his arms from the cold.

I quickly opened the door and he stepped into the house to stand in front of the fireplace.

"Lord Almighty, Cole. This is the coldest that I have ever seen up here in the wilds. It is so cold that I got Ross Huntsinger over at the barn with a pot bellied stove, just to keep our hosses from freezing."

Just then Laura peeked around the corner from the kitchen.

"Don't look, Judd, I'm going to dash to my room and get dressed."

Judd turned toward me and grinned. There were sounds of a quick scurry out of the kitchen and down the hall. A door swung shut and a muffled voice said,

"Lady! Keep your cold nose off of me."

Both Judd and I looked into each other's eyes, a grin formed on each of our faces. We could hardly contain ourselves. We had to cover our mouths to keep from laughing out loud. Momentarily, we moved to the kitchen for some of that hot coffee.

Laura quickly dressed in warm clothes and then after stomping her boots on, strode out to the kitchen where Judd and I sat talking with full cups of hot dark coffee.

"Good morning Judd. As soon as it gets lighter, I want to ride out to the north range and check on Sultan and his herd."

"Sure thing, Miss Laura. It's a good thing that we got that extra hay and feed this year, cause I think that this winter will be a humdinger."

"I agree. I want to bring Sultan in closer to the ranch. With weather this cold, every living thing will be either snuggled in for the winter or on the prowl for a meal. The wolves will be coming down from the high country and I sure don't want to provide fare for them."

We could not have known it at that time, but two days before and thirty-five hard miles north of the Sumner Ranch traveled a pitiful band of fifteen elderly Arapaho in search of food, shelter, and a fair hunting ground. They had become separated from their main band in a blinding blizzard while they escaped their reservation area.

Their Leader, Elk Heart, was up in years, but he still remembered the old ways. He knew that his band would have to find a safe place to camp and hunt—and it couldn't be too far away. He knew also, that the blue coat soldiers would pick up their trail and that they would be traveling fast and hard to catch them. He led his band south into the wild lower Colorado Territory where the going would be rough and treacherous.

A day's start behind them, young Lieutenant George Wesson led a troop of cavalry that surged forward through the snow. The chase was on. Lieutenant Wesson was a West Point graduate and it seemed that he had missed the great Indian Wars of the early 1870's. That idea nagged at his brain and now, he was out to show others on the frontier that he was the "best damn Indian fighter" in the West. A band of Arapaho had jumped their reservation and he was going to track them down and bring them back, dead or alive.

Also at around that same time, in a lonely cabin thirty some miles to the west of the center point between the Sumner Ranch and the trekking Arapaho, a young family felt the first pangs of illness.

Ted and Esther Roberts arrived in the wilds of the Lower Colorado only the year before with three small children, ages six, four, and two. They built themselves a small cabin and began to farm the land. They were a happy family content to live with the land and to enjoy nature to the fullest.

They had no way of knowing that on the eve of the wild blizzard, a lone white tailed deer staggered through the wilderness, infected with the Rocky Mountain Fever. The feverish animal slowly made its way on shaking legs to the riverbed and lowered its head to drink from the stream. It faltered and suddenly fell dead in the center of the stream. The clear cold creek water babbled over and around the carcass of the fallen deer and flowed downstream directly past the cabin built by Ted and Esther.

It was Esther that took sick first. She was mixing and kneading dough for fresh bread when she suddenly felt warm and nauseous. She shook her head. It was pounding with fever. She slipped to the floor. Immediately, the three children were by her side.

"Mommy!" They called out somewhat in unison. "What is the matter Mommy? Are you sick? How can we help?"

Esther turned to her eldest, a boy now of seven years. She swallowed dryly, then hoarsely whispered "Tommy, run and get your father. Tell him that I am sick. He must come right now."

Tommy ran out of the door, down the path to the creek bed where his father was fishing.

"Daddy! Come quick, Mommy has fallen down and she is awful sick."

Ted Roberts had been aching all over, and feeling poorly all morning himself. At Tommy's call, he stood up abruptly, then staggered and fell face down on the cold hard ground.

His son, Tommy knelt by his side.

"Help me up, Tommy. I have to get to your mother."

Tommy Roberts fought back the tears as he struggled to help his father to his feet. He felt helpless and inadequate for the task, but he kept on trying until Ted stood shakily and leaned on him for support. He helped his father slowly shuffle toward the cabin. Fifteen long minutes later, Ted Roberts stumbled into the cabin with Tommy alongside. He half dragged; half carried his wife to the bed. He feverishly managed to get her under the blankets, then collapsed onto the bed himself.

Weakly, he mumbled to his eldest child,

"Tommy. Mother and I are very sick. You will have to be the man of the house for a while and take care of your younger brother and sister. Make sure that there is lots of firewood. Keep the fireplace lit. Don't let it burn out. Get some cold water and keep a cool rag on our heads to break this fever. Keep us covered up so we can sweat this sickness out of us. Do that Tommy."

"I will Pa, I will."

Ted Roberts passed into a fever-weakened daze. He didn't know what he was saying; he didn't know where he was. He was only half-conscious to the world.

Tommy gathered his younger brother and three-year-old sister together.

"Mommy and Daddy are very sick. Don't worry, I will take care of you until they are better."

His brother, Jimmy, looked Tommy straight in the eyes and asked "But how can you take care of us? You are only seven years old Tommy."

Three year old Lisa spoke up. "I will ask baby Jesus to help us. He will send an angel to us. Mommy always says that when people are in trouble and need help, that Jesus sends an angel to help them."

Lisa walked over to the small hand carved nativity set in the corner, picked up the baby and cradled it tenderly in her arms. Her eyes were misty with worry for her parents. The two boys moved to her and they hugged. Tommy said with shaky voice,

"We will make it until mother and father are well. We just have to!"

I reckon that it was near to eight o'clock in the morning when Laura decided that they should wait no longer. She and five of her wranglers would ride out to the north range and haze her prize black stallion, Sultan, and his herd back toward the main ranch. Laura and the Sumner riders went to the stable for their mounts. Laura saddled up Mickey and I saddled up Warrior. We walked the horses outside into the main ranch yard and mounted.

I put boot to stirrup and swung into the saddle to ride up beside Laura. The nightmarish thoughts were still in my mind as I spoke to her.

"I'll ride along with you. I have an uneasy feeling in the pit of my stomach and it just don't set right. I'd feel better about it if I were along—just in case."

"I was hoping that you would come. Besides, Christmas is only a few days a way. By the way Cole, what did you get me this year?"

"Well, I got you the prettiest..." I caught myself just in time, "Wait a minute, you promised that there would be no leading questions. Now that is my secret. You'll just have to wait. By the way, just what did you get me?"

Laura held this pert little smile on her face as she answered me with "Sorry, Cole. A promise is a promise."

I thought then that a woman is always like that. They never say what they really mean. You know, if a man could figure out a woman he could make a million dollars just by selling the secret to other men that had no idea what their women were talking about. I sort of grinned with that notion. I laughed out loud a bit and suddenly found Laura looking intently at me, her head sort of cocked to one side.

"My secret thoughts."

She looked at me with those crystal blue eyes then. They held a look that told me that I wouldn't last long holding that secret. She was going to worm it out of me with her womanly ways. I was in trouble now.

No matter what kind of secret a man thinks he holds, if a woman gets wind of it, she is just naturally curious about it and she will file it in the back of her mind until one day, she will just casually let you answer her question. They have minds like—like—them elephants I heard about. They never forget.

Well, we made small talk as we rode along. We had gone close to twenty miles or so when we spotted movement in the distance. I suddenly had the feeling that I was going to be tested.

The movement grew larger until finally we could make out several figures moving in the snow. The closer they got, the better we saw what the situation was. It was a small ragged band of Indians. It turned out that they were all elderly people and they looked hungry. It was one of the most pitiful sights I had ever seen. These once proud people saw our group and decided to beg for food.

Laura, being the person she is, couldn't turn them down. She had her boys build a good fire and set up a hot meal for them. I looked at Laura and felt proud. Ever since I've known her, that being about two years now, she'd always been kind to those less fortunate.

It was about an hour later that the quiet peace of the moment was shattered by the not too distant jingle-jangling of a cavalry troop that came bustling down through the trees and sort of lined up like they was a going to war. I shore didn't like the looks of this, and I unbuttoned my heavy winter coat to put my Colt Revolver close to hand. For good measure, I pinned on my star and motioned to Laura. She knew exactly what I meant and placed her wranglers all around these people, Winchesters peaceably cradled in their arms.

The people looked up with fear in their eyes. Laura smiled at them and told them to continue their meal. She looked back to me as I was checking the loads in my Winchester.

Well, them boys in blue came a boiling on up to within ten feet of us. A slender young blonde haired officer smugly looked at those people and said,

"I am Lieutenant Wesson of the 2nd Cavalry. We have been trailing these hostiles for two days now. Thank you for capturing them. We will take them off your hands Sir."

I just looked directly into his peach fuzz face and said matter-of-factly "I think not, lieutenant. These people are not hostile. As a matter of fact, they are guests. Secondly, this land is within the bounds of the Sumner Ranch, of which you and your troop are trespassing. Thirdly, Miss Sumner there, the owner of this ranch, has hired all of these people to help hunt down and trap the wolves that plague her herds. I suggest that you turn your troop and go find the hostiles that you seek."

Well, that ruffled his feathers some. He got downright authoritative then and plainly stated for all to hear.

"I am an officer of the United States Army and my men will take those people now!"

A middle aged Sergeant quickly pushed his horse up to the Lieutenant and looked us both over. He grinned widely at me, and turning to the officer remarked,

"Lieutenant. You'd better do what this man says. You don't know who he is. I do. How are you today Marshal Stockton?"

"Afternoon, Clancy. It seems that we have a difference of opinion here. If the young man don't back off, then I'm going to arrest him."

The Lieutenant suddenly got quite indignant.

"Arrest me? I am the troop commander here. I demand those hostiles now".

"All right, lieutenant, You are under arrest for trespassing and conspiracy to incite a riot. Do you want to come peaceably or drag iron? Get down off that horse and surrender your side arms."

"Sergeant! Have the men draw carbines."

"No, Sir. I can't do that. Mr. Stockton is the **United States Marshal** for this territory and you, lieutenant are under arrest."

Well, that young gentleman's face was as white as a sheet. I will say that his cheeks were a bit rosy too. Must have been the cold.

"Well, Lieutenant. Do you get down off that horse or do I shoot you off it?"

He dismounted in a flurry of what I would call a v-e-r-y indignant manner.

It was just about that same moment that another troop of cavalry rode slowly and silently out of the opposite tree line and moved toward us. The lieutenant grinned widely.

"Now, Marshal, there are twice as many Army here. We will take charge."

The new troop drew closer and I saw that they were led by Spotted Hawk, a scout from Fort Lyon and Captain Starrett, an officer whom I met several months ago. Captain Starrett drew up to us and dismounted. Lieutenant Wesson snapped to attention and saluted smartly.

"Afternoon, Marshal Stockton. At ease, Lieutenant. Is there a problem here?"

"No problem, Captain. I just arrested your young lieutenant here for trespassing and inciting a riot."

"Captain Starrett, I chased these hostiles for over two days and now here they are. This civilian is denying our force to take charge of these hostiles, has threatened to shoot me, and has placed me under false arrest."

Captain Starrett turned to Spotted Hawk.

"Hawk, go talk to those people. Lieutenant, this is U.S. Marshal Cole Stockton. His word is law in this territory. If he says that you are under arrest, then you are under arrest. Cole, is that coffee I smell over on that fire? My men and I could sure could use a cup."

"Good idea, Captain. I always think better with a cup of coffee or two."

The two of us turned and walked to the fire, leaving the Lieutenant Wesson standing bewildered and wondering just what the devil was going on. Captain Starrett and I each filled us a cup with that steaming hot liquid.

"Damn, this is good coffee. How long you going to hold him, Cole?"

"Till he minds his manners."

"I thought as much. All right, you can have him for a week. With both troops under my command, we can track down the main band in that time."

I thought hard for a quick moment, then made a request.

"I would also like Spotted Hawk with me. There is something nagging at my mind that tells me his presence will make a difference in my present quest."

Captain Starrett studied my face for a moment before replying "Anything you want Marshal. I'll see you again in seven days."

Well, Laura did hire the small band of Arapaho to watch for wolves on her land. They were quite happy to have the chance to once again prove themselves *worthy*. She also directed them to a sheltered area of her land that they could operate from.

All was done through the interpreter talents of Spotted Hawk. At first, they were apprehensive. He then related to the small band, the great accomplishments of this "Woman Warrior" who rode like the wild Comanche from the south, who fought like the great Sioux from the north, and who was fearless in the face of death. They were all ears. The deal was struck in the ancient manner of handshakes and smoking of the pipe. I had to laugh when Laura's turn at the pipe came. I could've sworn that her face turned a little green when she sucked up on that tobacco.

Lieutenant Wesson looked very forlorn as he watched his troop ride out to look for the main hostile band under the command of Captain Starrett. You could easily see that he sorely wanted to be with them when they caught up to the main group. Yet, he still showed an obstinate side to his person. Well, perhaps taking him along on this journey would mellow him out. I certainly hoped so.

Laura gave instructions to her wranglers to continue on to the north section and work Sultan and his herd back toward the main ranch. Then, she looked thoughtfully at me.

"I think that I want to go with you, Spotted Hawk, and the Lieutenant. Something deep inside tells me that I need to be with you. Maybe I need to find the source of this nightmare also for resolution."

"That's fine Laura, but I don't know exactly where I am going yet. I just know that somewhere fairly close by, there is someone that needs my help. I am just moving on a hunch, but there are some new families out toward the west of here that I haven't met yet. I figure to stop by and introduce myself."

We four waited until the last of our group had departed. Then we swung into the saddle and started toward the west and the wild slopes of the Colorado Rocky Mountains. Spotted Hawk shook his head approvingly. He swung in beside Lieutenant Wesson and began to point out the interests of nature.

I couldn't help but smile a bit. This young officer was about to get an education not afforded in even the best schools of the east. Four hours later, Spotted Hawk had the officer repeating the Indian names for various animals, trees, and even waving his hands in different shapes and moves. I figured it out. Spotted Hawk was teaching Lieutenant Wesson to speak in the universal language of "sign".

I'll say this. The young man seemed to relax a bit and he was definitely a fast learner. He almost looked like he was enjoying it. Well, time would tell.

We found the first homestead and it was deserted. I'd said many a time before, that it takes a special love of the land to stick it out. Some folks think that they are in heaven when they first arrive in the territory, but after a few months of hardship they pack up and move on—always looking for their niche in the world. We halted there for a quick fire, some jerky, biscuits, and coffee.

We moved on further to the west. Two more hours ride brought us to the next homestead. This one was occupied by a middle-aged couple named John and Cassie Middleton. They welcomed us into their home and treated us to hot coffee, a warm fire, and some freshly baked holiday cookies. After that, the Middleton's invited us to spend the night with them. Having covered some good ground, we accepted their kind invitation. We had supper with our hosts after unsaddling and turning our mounts into their newly constructed stable.

It was the quiet moments of the night after everyone else had drifted off into slumber that Laura snuggled close to me whispering "Cole, I still have those feelings and they are stronger than ever. They make me shiver with cold. Hold me close."

I knew what she felt. I had the same feelings, and the sense of urgency was even greater than before. I slipped into another fitful slumber while portions of the dream once again filtered across my mind. It was then that the wind suddenly picked up. It began with a low moan then transitioned into a wild howl. Snow came with it. Another blizzard. The temperatures dipped into the twenty below mark. It was not a fit night for man nor beast.

As we were spending the stormy night with our gracious hosts, several hours away sat the cabin that we sought nestled amongst a stand of pines. Three children sat in the dimness of a low burning fireplace bundled together while speaking softly to each other.

It was the third night since the fever started and the parents were hanging on but mostly unconscious and filled with the sickness. The children kept the fireplace going until the last heap of firewood now sat at the hearth. They began to feed it sparingly—the cold began to seep into the cabin. The children covered their parents with as many blankets as they could spare, then huddled together around the fireplace. Tommy had opened yet another can of beans with the hunting knife and after warming it on the hearth, he divided the beans into thirds and cut some bread. The children ate and then he washed off the dishes as best that he could.

The children talked about stories that their Mother had told them. They talked about the miracles of the Lord. They talked about baby Jesus in Bethlehem. They talked of the miracle of the *Star.*

It was in the middle of the night and the low coals of the fireplace cast an eerie light in the small cabin. All were asleep except for little Lisa. She clutched the small doll from the nativity scene to her and closed her brown eyes tightly. She whispered "Dear Jesus. Please help us. Mommy and Daddy are very sick and it is so cold in our house. We have almost no food left. Please help us."

She closed her eyes and in one brief second a quick vision crossed her mind. Suddenly, her eyes popped open and she smiled as she thought to herself,

"Jesus is sending a shiny "*Star*" and an "*Angel*" to help us." Lisa closed her eyes then, snuggling close to her brothers for the warmth. She held an almost angelic smile on her face as she drifted off into a world of peaceful dreams.

It was early the next morning after a hearty breakfast of hotcakes, maple syrup, deer steak strips, and plenty of that freshly ground dark coffee that our small party mounted up to continue our quest.

Laura spoke soothingly to Mickey and Spotted Hawk spoke soothingly to his mount before swinging up into the saddle. I just put boot to stirrup and when I set myself into the saddle, Warrior took several good hops that I was unprepared for.

Laura laughed gaily and Spotted Hawk closed his eyes and turned away, out of politeness I guess. That young lieutenant threw back his head and roared. He roared with laughter, that is, until his bottom hit the saddle of his own horse. Then the two of us were bucking all around John and Cassie's yard. It was a mighty fine display of horse displeasure.

Warrior finally settled down. I guess that he didn't like that cold saddle just as much as I didn't like sitting on it. The young Officer finally got his mount calmed down and with a friendly wave, we rode out toward the next homestead on my mind.

This homestead was situated in a small clearing amongst some pines along a nice stretch of creekbed as I recalled. There was land enough for the plow and a small family could live there comfortably by raising their own garden produce supplemented with a bit of hunting and fishing. It would be near to late afternoon before we reached that clearing.

Once again, Spotted Hawk was pointing out the beauties of nature to the young officer. Laura and I rode together, our eyes searching the wilderness for any sense of our foreboding thoughts.

It was near to five or six in the evening when I called a halt and raising up in the saddle I inhaled of the crisp air. There were two scents that struck me. The first was the chill of the air filled with frozen mist. Another blizzard was right in front of us, coming in fast. The second was the unmistakable scent of wood-smoke—kind of thin, but it was undoubtedly woodsmoke.

That homestead was only a mile or so ahead. We moved forward and within minutes the wind began to howl like a wild cougar in the night. The flurries suddenly appeared out of no where and the temperature dropped almost thirty degrees.

We faced straight into that storm and the icy wind frosted our faces and bodies something fierce. Our heads hung low in attempts to gain some kind of shelter from the icy blast.

It was only when Warrior and Mickey suddenly stopped in their tracks and refused to take another step that Laura and I looked to the side. There it was, the cabin. We both shivered hard and turned the horses to the dark and ominous sight. There was a stable to the right of the cabin and we made for it. Upon entering, we stripped our gear off the horses. I asked Spotted Hawk and Lieutenant Wesson to rub down all the animals. They agreed.

Laura and I made our way to the cabin door. I rapped on it solidly, calling out to the inhabitants, "Hello there! U.S. Marshal. Is anyone here?"

It was only a minute before the door opened slowly. Laura was the first to enter and I was right behind her. She stopped in her tracks. I moved up behind her and letting my eyes accustom to the dimness, I too, took in the scene.

Three haggard looking children were huddled together, wrapped up and shivering under one thin blanket. The coals of the fireplace were almost out. There was no firewood to be seen at all. One child, a little girl, looked up at Laura and smiled,

"See! Here is our *Angel*. Isn't she beautiful?"

Laura rushed up to the children and asked them where their parents were. They pointed to the next room. Laura dashed into the room and suddenly I heard her say, "Cole! Come quick, these people are very sick."

I moved quickly into that room. Both parents were covered with blankets but still shaking with fever.

"Laura, take some of them blankets off the parents and wrap it around those children. I'll get Spotted Hawk in here. The lieutenant and I will get some wood. That fire has got to get started again or we'll all freeze."

I dashed out of the cabin back to the stable and quickly explained the situation to both. Spotted Hawk grabbed up his saddlebags among other strange wares and made for the cabin. The lieutenant and I grabbed up an axe as we headed for some wood. We grabbed up all of the dry wood that we could find. We even pulled planks off of the stable in some areas to at least get that fire going again.

We carried our gear into the cabin as well. Laura had gotten that cast iron stove going. She dragged out a large pot and began building a delicious hot mulligan stew (meaning that anything and everything that was edible was thrown into the pot). A large pot of freshly ground coffee was also started, much to my liking.

Within minutes, Lieutenant Wesson and I had a large blazing fire going in that hearth. The aroma of that fine stew and coffee began to fill the cabin. The lieutenant and I finally took off our heavy winter coats and set them down in a corner. Suddenly, the little girl looked up at me and pointed at my Marshal's Badge saying, "See there! That is the **Star** that I dreamed about and Miss Laura is the **Angel** that I dreamed about. See, Jesus sent them to help us."

Spotted Hawk called me into the adjoining room.

"These people have Mountain fever. It is very bad. It comes from something infected—maybe animal they eat, maybe skins they wear or maybe even water they drink. We must find this infection and kill it. I have given these people much strong medicine. They sleep easy now—maybe as much as two days. They will be strong with good food, rest, and plenty of good water to drink. I will go down to the creek and get some."

The next thing that I knew, Laura was sitting on the floor in the middle of those children and telling them stories of horses—wrangling them, taming them, and riding them. The children were all ears. I sort of smiled to myself. Laura had the most beautiful aura about her—yah, almost like an Angel. I pondered on that a while.

The lieutenant minded the fire and kept it burning even and controlled in the hearth so that an even flow of warmth spread across the room. He looked like he was enjoying himself. He too, was listening to the stories.

Spotted Hawk came back from the creek with the fresh water. He was dipping it into some cups when he abruptly stopped pouring it and began to smell it. He then stuck his finger into the icy cold clear liquid and then tasted it. He shook his head.

"Mar-shal, this water bad, very bad. It smell like sickness, it taste very much like old animal blood. Maybe this reason for the people sickness, we must find out. We must ride upstream until we find what makes the water bad."

"Hawk, you are the Medicine Man here. You stay. Lieutenant, get your coat, we are going for a ride."

We saddled up and slowly worked our way up both sides of that creek. It was a long and tedious task due to the thickness of the bushes along the way. Continued snow flurries didn't help much either.

Finally, six miles up stream we found it, the partially decomposed carcass of a deer. It was eaten badly by worms and maggots and all around it, a sort of mucus was flowing from the remains. I let out my lariat and taking a swing or two looped it around them antlers, tying my end to the saddle horn. Warrior dragged the soggy carcass out of the stream. The carcass would have to be burned. We dragged it back to the cabin area where we would pile and pyre it with enough wood to burn it to ashes. First, we needed coffee and food.

We re-stabled the horses and made our way to the cabin. Laura had those children sitting around their makeshift table devouring that stew like a bunch of wild horse wranglers.

The lieutenant went back to his fireplace duties along with a big bowl of that stew and a cup of that hot coffee. I conferred with Spotted Hawk. He shook his head up and down.

"Yes, that would do it. We must burn that deer. If any other animal eats of its flesh, it too will become infected. We must hurry and build the funeral. It must burn very hot—very sure. Pour coal oil on the animal so that it catches very quickly".

After eating up two large bowls of Laura's stew, devouring several large biscuits, and drinking two cups of coffee, the lieutenant and I built up the funeral pyre. We set to cremating the carcass. The pyres burned through the evening and into the midnight hour. We watched it burn until there was nothing more than a pile of glowing ash in the dirt.

Afterward, approaching the cabin, we thought that we heard voices. They were singing. We drew nearer and now we could make them out. There were children singing Christmas songs. I sort of smiled to myself as I remembered my own family sitting around the fireplace on Christmas Eve drinking a warm beverage and singing a favorite song or two. I glanced toward Lieutenant Wesson. His eyes were soft. I wouldn't swear to it, but I thought that they held a bit of mist. We stopped at the door, hesitating a bit before entering.

The cabin held a soft glow from the smoldering coals, plenty of firewood was stacked to the side of the hearth, the children lay wrapped in warm blankets toward a corner and were settling down for the night.

Laura had arranged our gear together. Spotted Hawk had arranged George Wesson's as well as his own gear in positions for warmth around the fire.

We each poured another cup of coffee and looked into each other's eyes. It was Laura that spoke our thoughts, "Do you know what this night is? It is Christmas Eve. These children have no gifts. What are we going to do about it?"

Spotted Hawk spoke, "I can make Indian music flute. I will make two for the boys."

The lieutenant spoke, his head lowered a bit, but grinning at the thought, "Give me an old sock, some sewing material, thread, a pen and ink, and a needle. I can make rag dolls. I—I used to make them for my younger sister."

Laura spoke. "I will bake some holiday cookies. I think that there is enough flour, sugar, and other things to do that. What will you give, Cole? What can a man like you give to children?"

"I don't know, Laura. I will have to think on that. In the meantime, you all do like you said."

I turned away and pulling on my heavy coat, stepped outside into the cold. I sighed heavily, then reached into my inside pocket to produce the makings. I rolled myself a smoke whilst I thought long and hard about just what a gunfighter and U.S. Marshal could give a child.

I decided to walk around a bit and I found myself looking into the now clear, cold sky at them millions of stars. I asked myself again and again just what was it that a man like me could give children that would be worthwhile to them.

After all, Laura was baking cookies. That was worthwhile. Laura's cookies were pretty much bragged on by her wranglers. Spotted Hawk could whittle on wood and make something worthwhile. Lieutenant Wesson could make dolls, and that was an invaluable gift for little girls.

Just what was it that I could do to make it a good Christmas for these children?

I looked once again into the heavens at them twinkling stars. Suddenly, it came to me. It was a modest gift, but one which I could readily bestow. I nodded my head and turned back to the cabin. I knew exactly what I could give.

"Well, Cole? Did you think of something?"

"Yes, Laura. It ain't much, but it's all I got. I need a pen and a piece of paper."

We rummaged them up and I sat there at that small kitchen table writing some words upon that paper. When I was finished, I let Laura read it. She got the biggest smile on her face that I had ever seen and nodded her head approvingly.

It was only a few hours before dawn that they all placed their gifts in the stockings hanging from the fireplace. I held onto mine. We slipped silently into our bedrolls and with a long sigh, tried to get some sleep.

Laura snuggled up to me and I turned to face her. "Merry Christmas." she whispered to me and I whispered it back to her. I closed my eyes as she melted into my arms and I felt the warmth of her soul surround me. A sense of peace entered my mind and together we drifted off into a land of sweet dreams. The horror of before had vanished.

In another corner of the homestead cabin, a little girl smiled in her sleep. She was warm, she was fed, her quiet prayer had been fulfilled. The promise of a guiding *Star* and an *Angel* was fulfilled. Her parents were given medicine for the fever and it was said that they would recover soon.

It was Christmas morning and the air was chilled. A blanket of newly laid snow afforded a scenic panorama of wintry splendor all across the lower Colorado.

Three children slowly rose from their warm blankets to find a smiling Army officer tending the hearth, a smiling old Indian nodding his head, a beautiful woman wearing boots and Levi's, and a man with a *Shiny Star* on his vest grinning like he had just raided a cookie jar.

Spotted Hawk raised his knowing finger toward the stockings hung on the mantle. The children's eyes followed his every move and their eyes widened in sheer disbelief. They recovered their stockings and the boys found whistles that worked. Lisa found a beautiful rag doll and hugged it to her. They looked to the table and found a large platter of holiday cookies. All of the children beamed with pleasure.

Suddenly, stirring noises came from the next room. Moans and then, followed by,

"What am I doing here? I should be watching my supper cook."

Spotted Hawk moved toward the room and stuck his head around the corner.

A shrill shriek sounded as a woman screamed out. Laura leaped up and ran into the room with Spotted Hawk. There were quick, soft words and after several minutes, Esther Roberts appeared in the main room of the cabin on shaky legs and held up by Laura. Laura led her to sit with her children. Eyes misted as the children hugged their mother and planted kisses on her cheek.

Several long minutes later, Ted Roberts turned over and fell out of the bed. Spotted Hawk and Lieutenant Wesson gathered him up and brought him to sit with his family. Once again, hugs and love were spread.

Laura nudged me at that moment and I knew that I had to give my gift to the children. I sort of hung my head in thought, then unfolded the piece of paper that I wrote on. I began,

"It has come to my attention that in the face of overwhelming odds, these young people performed life giving service to their parents. It is justly so, that I, Cole Stockton, U.S. Marshal, Lower Colorado Territory, do hereby administer the Oath and appoint each of these young persons to be "Honorary" Deputy United States Marshals. For most people the Star of authority means the law of the gun, for you, however, it means that you have saved lives, and that is the true meaning of this day—Christmas."

I looked at each of them and with a wide grin on my face and said,

"Raise yore right hands and swear after me, I…do solemnly swear to uphold the laws of the United States of America, so help me GOD."

Three children stood quietly while I pinned on each of them, a Deputy U.S. Marshal's Star. Somehow I figured that the U.S. Marshal's Office could afford to pay the unheard of sum of "one dollar per month" per Deputy for at least a year. I would see to it with Judge Wilkerson.

I would remember the "hug" that little Lisa gave me for a long, long time.

To sum it up, Laura's Sultan was very smart. He was halfway back to the main ranch when the wranglers caught up with him—in fact, he led them to the ranch. Young Lieutenant Wesson was very humble, but very enriched with experience when I released him from arrest. He and Spotted Hawk rode together toward Fort Lyon.

As for Laura and I? W-e-l-l, it was probably the greatest gift that a man and a woman could ever give each other. Our love for each other, sealed with a smoldering kiss.

The time of Christmas is giving. Giving something of yourself is a giving that stands time. There are them that give gifts costing a bit of money. There are those that spend their own time and effort to produce a gift. I figure that amongst all, those from the heart are best received. Those from our own thoughts and abilities are definitely received and most cherished. To this end, I submit the following,

∽

"May the Good Lord take you by the hand and lead you to the waters of eternal peace. It is my wish for all.

MERRY CHRISTMAS and a prosperous New Year.

"STAR OF PEACE"

You could tell that it was that time of year again. Children were behaving mighty well, and folks seemed to have a bit more tolerance for each other. That made my job quite a bit easier. Being the United States Marshal, I was quite often the first person that folks looked for when trouble was a foot, and for some, the last person they wanted to meet. Whichever way that fate chose, I was bound by personal oath to keep the peace and sometimes that proved to be quite a chore.

It was only a few days before Christmas when I rode into town and dismounted in front of the jail. The air was crisp and although the area was still a bit sparse of snow, you could tell that we were in for a white carpeted holiday.

Folks were hustling and bustling all around the town in search of the perfect gifts. The General Store was doing a booming business. The Lower Colorado Ladies Society League obtained some festive bunting and solicited "volunteers", namely their husbands, to string decorations up all over town.

A festive Christmas ball was advertised on some hand drawn posters tacked up here and there around the town, and it suddenly dawned on me that the light shining in Laura's eyes lately was centered around us attending that ball.

Now, I don't claim to be the best dancer in the world, nor in the Territory of the Lower Colorado. As a matter of fact, I was probably the worst of all ballroom "stompers". Yet, I recalled that the last time I danced with Laura, I felt like I was in seventh heaven.

We made quite a dashing couple. I must've stepped on her feet a dozen times, but she didn't say anything. She just leaned against me, and looked at me with those smoldering blue eyes, a smile on her face. I'd held her close to me and suddenly, all those lonely years faded from my mind. I was, in fact, somewhat speechless. The feelings that passed between us though as we gazed into each other's eyes were something to behold. I found myself mesmerized by her thoughts as they filtered across my mind and a certain understanding passed between us. Here was a woman that put me at ease with myself, as well as stirred my blood.

During quiet moments, we would look at each other and I felt a certain softness that drowned out the haunting memories of well over two dozen gunfights with hard bitten men of vicious temper, and of lonely times on wild, dangerous trails. It was during these times, together, that I felt at peace with myself, and know'd that the good Lord had saved my bacon a time or two for something special.

Laura and I would attend that ball, and I could hardly wait to see her decked out in one of her finest dresses. She always made me proud to stand with her, and I hoped that she felt the same.

As far as a Christmas gift for Laura, I had not yet found a thing that I felt that she could use, or want. I had faith in myself though, and would keep looking and thinking on it. Just what do you give a woman who seemingly has everything?

❧   ❧   ❧

Laura Sumner glided lightly around her kitchen humming a gay holiday tune to herself. She had her apron on, but nevertheless had smidgens of flour along her cheeks and forehead. She had been baking cookies, pies, and cinnamon rolls all day while she thought of the gift she had gotten for Cole Stockton, and of the upcoming Christmas Ball in town.

"Cole will be pleased." she thought pleasantly to herself.

Laura had thought long and hard on what Cole might like for Christmas, and finally it came to her. She was browsing through all of the mail order catalogs in the General Store one day in early October when she saw the advertisement.

> "A modern man needs a timepiece that is correct in every sense. This piece is magnificently fashioned with precise Swiss movement, guaranteed for a lifetime of accurate time keeping. This purchase includes a gold casing with initials of your choice. A one and half foot gold chain with fob is included."

It would be the perfect gift for Cole, especially since he had no accurate way to tell time. Like most men of the frontier, he looked at the sun, the moon, the stars, and guessed the approximate time of day. Now he would be able to tell precisely what time it was. Yes, Cole would love this gift.

Laura filled out the order form and attached a bank draft for the entire amount of fifty dollars. The order would take six weeks to arrive. That would be just in time for the holidays. Laura was extremely proud of herself.

"I wonder what Cole is getting me this time?" she thought. I just know that it will be something special.

Laura's momentary thoughts were suddenly interrupted by a knock at the front door. She opened it to admit Judd Ellison and Juan Soccorro. They had been to the hills and selected a beautiful yellow pine for her Christmas tree.

Laura showed them where to put it. She had her box of decorations already out and sitting on the sofa. The boys shed their heavy winter coats and began to string garland and place ornaments on the tree.

"Gee, Miss Laura, that coffee sure smells good, and those cinnamon rolls too."

Laura smiled. "Help yourself boys, but leave some for later."

They eagerly helped themselves to a steaming cup of coffee and a couple of her rolls. This is what Christmas was all about for Laura's wranglers. They loved the delicious baked goods that Laura always came up with. Although an excellent horsewoman, she was also quite a cook.

❧   ❧   ❧

Sheriff J.C. Kincaid and I were sitting in the jail enjoying a fresh cup of coffee when the large painted wagon pulled up in front. A man climbed down from the wagon and stepped up to the jail door.

"Howdy", he said as he entered and closed the door behind him.

He was rather tall, gray haired, and dressed in a dark suit with white shirt and dark blue satin tie. He wore a tall black hat.

"I am looking for the local authority for this town. I am Doctor Joseph Quintmire and I would like to set up my traveling medicine show and sales in your fair city. This is our last stop before heading to the warmer climates of New Mexico, Arizona and the like. I have tonics for just about everything that ails the body, a magic show, gypsy fortune teller, and the best man with firearms the world has ever seen. There is no target too small or too far away for him to hit. His skill is second to none. Why, he can even outshoot Buffalo Bill Cody, that famous marksman. What does it take to set up my show in this town?"

I immediately thought, "Now, this is something I have got to see."

J.C. Kincaid looked at me questioningly.

"It's your town, J.C. Whatever you decide."

"O.K. You can set up at the outskirts of town. I must warn you though. If I detect any foul play, I will close your outfit down. I will not have my citizens taken in by fraud."

"My dear Sheriff. We are law abiding people, of that you can rest assured. We will abide by your rules and conduct our small show accordingly. Your citizens will enjoy themselves immensely."

The good Doctor departed to his wagon, and I was grinning.

"Go ahead and say it Cole. I really put my foot in it this time—didn't I."

"I don't know, J.C., I don't know. I will help you watch the situation though. Some of these medicine shows can get out of hand yet others are pretty fair entertainment. Besides, I want to see this feller who can outshoot Bill Cody. Let's just watch and see which way it goes."

It was the next day that Laura and I rode into town on her ranch wagon together. Warrior trailed behind. That traveling medicine show was all set up and in full bloom. There was a fairly large crowd gathered around it, and Laura wanted to stop, look, and listen for a while. I agreed.

Doc Quintmire was a talking up a storm about his concoctions and telling everyone there that it would cure everything from dandruff to aches and pains. He sold quite a few bottles of that elixir at a buck a bottle. Next came the magic show.

Some foreign looking feller stood out on the small stage and did some card tricks. I wondered then as to what kind of gambler he would make. Then he tied knots in some lengths of rope and would you believe it, them knots just seemed to disappear. It was magic. The last thing he did was to pull doves from his seemingly empty hat and released them into the air. The crowd loved this act. So far, I could spot nothing amiss.

Well, Laura being the curious woman that she is, just had to have her fortune read by the gypsy woman. I told her that I would wait for her beside the show stage. I wanted to see that feller shoot and it wasn't long before Ole Doctor Quintmire stood before the crowd and announced, "Ladies and Gentlemen! Here he is! The one! The only! Johnny Blackstone! Johnny Blackstone is the fastest, most accurate, marksman in the world."

Well, he stepped out to the platform, and was he duded up! He wore a totally bleached set of fringed buckskins with shinny black boots and silver

Well, he swept off that hat again and bowed like a knight in the king's court. I found myself somewhat embarrassed. Never in my life had I the faintest idea that I would be someone's ideal. I looked out over the crowd and there was J.C. Kincaid and Laura standing together. Both had wide grins on their faces. I flushed again.

I shook hands with the young man, and stepped down offen that stage to hand clapping and yahoo's from the crowd. I didn't know it then, but this young man's presence was going to stir up some holiday trouble.

❧   ❧   ❧

After that show, I walked down to the General Store with Laura. She was needing some more baking ingredients, for one. Seems them wranglers, no matter how they tried, just couldn't keep their mitts offen her baked goods. Laura scolded them to their face, but underneath, she was just smiling kind of proud like. They were like little kids when it came to fresh baked cookies, pies, and cinnamon rolls. In a way, I sort of dreaded being in her company at the General Store.

I knew what was on her mind, and it involved the question of what did I get her for Christmas. Well, here it was only two days to go, and I hadn't a clue. Maybe, I thought, she will take particular attention to something, and I will sneak back and get it for her. No such luck. The only attention she paid was to the amount of flour, sugar, cinnamon, yeast, coffee, and apples that the clerk piled up on the counter.

I thought that I would wander around the store and just browse. I saw a few interesting things, but when I looked around, there was Laura watching me out of the corners of her eyes. No, there was just nothing that appealed to me as something really special for a real special lady. I was frazzled about this whole thing.

I mean that Laura owns a horse ranch. She has a wagon, she has horses, she has guns, she has chaps, spurs, and saddles. She has all the cooking utensils that she needs. She has a good pair of riding boots. She has some pretty fancy dresses, as well as working outfits of jeans, shirts, bandanas, and a couple of hats—not to mention her "lucky" black Stetson. What in the world would she need, or want? Well, I would keep on looking and thinking.

We finished at the General Store, and walked side by side down to the Town Hall. That was where the Christmas Ball was to be held.

spurs. He had a wide brimmed white hat to match the color of those fringe buckskins.

Johnny Blackstone couldn't have been older than twenty-two, but he was sporting a fancy brace of matched nickel plated Colt .45 Revolvers with antler grips and carrying a Winchester '73.

Some men placed bull's eye targets at various intervals toward the open end of town, and the last target at about one hundred yards. The young shooter had one member of the crowd yell "Go!" and he fairly well drilled each and every one of those bulls eyes dead center with that Winchester.

Next, he had a woman from the crowd throw a hand full of silver dollars into the air. He drew them Colts and hit each and every one of those coins. I had to admit it. It was a sight of shooting. The young man swept off his hat and bowed low to the exuberant crowd and I guess that no one was quite prepared for what happened next.

Just to prove his point, he issued a challenge for any taker to try and match his skill. As he was explaining the rules, some men were placing two sets of empty whiskey bottles along a fence rail. Well, there were a couple of takers to his challenge.

He fairly outshot all five of them. He was quicker, and more accurate, and I was enjoying the show, when some rascal in the crowd yelled out that maybe the U.S. Marshal should try his luck. I sort of flushed with the notion.

Well, the majority of the crowd chanted along with expectations and I suddenly found myself standing next to this young stranger.

He would take the left six and I would take the right six whiskey bottles. Someone yelled "Draw" and both of us went for the targets. I have to say that it was pretty close. Both of us got six out of six at almost the same time.

The kid eyed me with almost unbelieving looks. I guessed that he had never met a real gunfighter before. Well, he just had to prove himself, so, the next thing out've his mouth was to shoot the remaining neck pieces. We reloaded and the men placed the two-inch bottle neck remnants along the fence rail.

Round two was almost the same result, except I was a mite quicker this time. It was then that he turned to me and asked my name.

"Cole Stockton." I replied, kind of sheepishly.

"My God. I don't believe it! I have read stories of you in almost all of the Eastern papers as well as some dime novels. Now I have finally met you. It was those stories about you that prompted me to want to be the best with firearms that I could be. I bow to you Sir."

The tickets were on sale and just fifty cents each. You should have seen how her eyes lit up with pure delight when I forked over the money for two tickets. Laura also went and signed up for the potluck. She would provide two chocolate cakes, and I could about just taste them.

Looking at the sign up list, I found that a couple of the best hunters signed up to bag some wild turkeys. That would sure hit the spot. There was sure to be some baked yams, beans, cobbed corn, and maybe even some light, fluffy biscuits and fresh homemade bread, not to mention a lot of freshly churned butter.

I figured that I would have to watch that punch bowl though. I remembered the punch bowl incident at the Lower Colorado Ladies Society welcome for Laura's cousin, Victoria, a few months back, and I chuckled a mite. It seemed that some good-natured boys had spiked the punch with some Texas down home tequila and it took a few of us for surprise. Anyway, Laura looked at me like I had lost my senses—me, laughing at seemingly nothing.

There was a definite frost in the air as we walked back to her ranch wagon and I helped load it up. I looked up at the sun and it seemed that there was a misty halo around it. That was a sure sign to me that some mighty cold temperatures were on the way.

Anyway, Laura would drive the ranch wagon back and I would stay in town for a bit longer. Warrior had trailed the wagon into town, just in case of situations like this. I never knew when something might come up and I would have to ride out to quell some kind of trouble.

I watched her drive out of town, and then took Warrior down to the jail stable. I unsaddled him, rubbed him down a mite, and gave him an extra bait of grain.

J.C. Kincaid was pouring himself a cup of fresh coffee when I entered the jail. I grabbed up a cup of that strong black liquid myself, and we talked a bit. He relayed his thoughts about the traveling medicine show and so far, he hadn't found anything amiss. Folks were having fun, just like old Doc Quintmire had said they would.

"So, Cole, how's it feel to be a real hero?"

"Aw, J.C., it's kind of embarrassing. You know how those dime novels and Eastern news accounts are. They only tell half the truth, and then stretch the living daylights out of that. Besides, I have a feeling that kid has never been west of the Mississippi until now."

"Yeah, Cole, but he sure put you to the test with them bottles."

"Well, J.C., bottles are one thing, but hard-bitten men are another. It was easy to shoot them bottles. That's how I learned, but the hardest lessons came later."

I sort of reflected back then to my earlier years. I had occasion to defend myself against the guns of some men whom I had once considered friends. They had turned bad, and I decided against joining them. It was a hard thing for me to do but, it was my life or theirs. It was that shooting that set me to traveling the wild and lonely trails, and to never get close to anyone again. That is, until lately.

The first time that I looked into Laura Sumner's crystal blue eyes there was a certain feeling deep within me. It was the feeling of restful peace. Just being around her put me at ease with myself, and the memories faded from view.

The more I got to know her, the more respect I had for her, and to tell the truth, the more I longed to hold her in my arms. It was like she was a piece of myself—down deep in my soul. I reckon that some folks would call it love. For us, though, it was an unspoken mutual understanding that she was my woman, and I would look after her the best that I could.

My thoughts were sharply interrupted just then. Jim Morton, one the hands at the Lazy "J" stepped into the office.

"Sheriff Kincaid, Marshal Stockton! You better step over to the medicine show. A couple of real rough hombres rode into town, and one of them is trying to goad that young feller into a REAL gunfight. That hardcase is packing two guns low and tied down. The kid looks real nervous about it, and folks are backing off to give them some space."

"Let's go J.C.", and as an afterthought, I said "And bring that shotgun." We went out the door and down the street to the edge of town. The two drifters had spread out and were facing that young man. They were so intent on calling him out that they didn't notice J.C. and I come up behind them.

"Howdy fellers. I understand that you want a real gunfight. How about trying me?"

That sort of startled them. One of the men looked back over his shoulder and the look on his face could have churned buttermilk. He went ashen.

"A-h-h, Gary, that is Cole Stockton behind you, and he looks like he means business."

Gary Swain never looked back at me. I knew him and he knew me. "Stay out've this Stockton. This here is between me and the kid. He says that he is the fastest and most accurate, and I want him to prove it. I say that he is yeller, and won't draw against the likes of me."

"Just stand easy Gary. There will be no gunplay right now. I want to speak to the kid for a moment."

Well, there it was. This was the wilds. This was gun country, and when a man got called out, he was bound to go, else he be known as a coward wherever he went. This was the unwritten Law of the West and I had no call to interfere, except to see that both men had an equal chance, and to see to the burying of the loser. I walked up to the kid and looked him straight in the eye.

"You ever shot at a man before?"

"No Sir. I never shot at a man before in my whole life."

"Well, the fats in the fire now. You are going to have to shoot at him, because he is going to shoot at you."

"Marshal, I can't do it. I can't shoot at a man, only targets."

"Maybe we can save this day after all" I said, "Listen to me", and I softly spoke to him so that the others couldn't hear my words. He agreed. Then I turned to Gary Swain. "O.K. Gary, you can shoot it out. Where shall I send your body?"

Gary just looked at me. His eyes were questioning now. I just grinned at him.

"O.K. Boys, when I say go, both of you draw. May the best man win."

J.C. Kincaid looked at me like I had lost all of my senses. I motioned him back, then moved out of the line of fire myself. Well those boys just stood there glaring at each other for the longest time. I took my time about it because I wanted Gary to sweat a bit.

Finally, I yelled, "Go!" Both men flashed for their revolvers and three shots split the afternoon silence. The crowd went wide-eyed. J.C. put it quite simple, "Well, I'll be dammed."

The kid outdrew Gary and his first shot severed Gary's right hand holster. The second shot severed his left hand holster, and the third sailed Gary's Stetson high into the air. Both of Gary Swain's holsters had dropped to the ground, with Gary's revolvers still in them. Now that was some fancy shooting.

Gary, of course was red faced, and a bit shaken. I didn't blame him much. He just quietly shook his head and apologized to the kid. Both of the men mounted and rode out of town amid a silence. J.C. Kincaid came up to me and asked,

"Just what did you say to that kid?"

"Well, he told me that he had never shot a man before, so I told him to shoot at targets, targets that would forego a gunfight. I knew that he was fast enough. He just needed some direction, and Gary's gunbelt was obviously a good target. Besides, the kid is going back East on the next stage."

Putting on a sharp shooter show is great business back east, but out here, someone may just call you on it. The kid learned that point quickly and made the right decision.

J.C. decided to stop in at the Lady Luck Saloon to see Louise Montrose, and I walked back to the jail for some more of that hot coffee.

❧   ❧   ❧

I had just settled down in one of those wooden high backed chairs when the jailhouse door opened and Dooley Jergens staggered in. I could smell the odor of whiskey on him from across the room.

"Highsh, Marshal. Well, heresh I am. Good. Shave you the…hic…trouble of…hic…carrying me to the jail. I am drunk and I demand to be locked up before my woman comes into town and beats the tar outten me."

"Just how many often do you get drunk, Dooley?" I asked.

"Only onceit a year, Marshal. Every day before Christmas Eve. I got six young kids to do Christmas fer, and it is a chore in itself. I got to be sober on Christmas Day so's I can put them red flannels on and fake beard to be Santa fer them and pass out gifts, such as they are. Well, are you going to lock me up?"

I grinned. "O.K., Dooley just walk back to the cell and I'll be there directly after I finish my coffee. Just lay down on the cot and don't worry none."

It was within the hour that Mrs. Jergens came to the jail in search of her man, Dooley.

She was a fairly slim woman with big brown eyes and light brown hair. Her face and hands were tanned somewhat and I surmised that she worked a garden at home. She wore the usual garb of a farmer's wife, calico dress, shawl and flowered bonnet.

"Good afternoon, Marshal. I come to check on my man, Dooley. I supposed that he has indulged in his yearly spree and is sleeping it off in your jail. He does this every year, the day before Christmas Eve. I hope he didn't put you out none. He is a good man and works hard on our farm. He deserves at least one day out on the town a year".

"You are not mad at him?"

"Oh, of course not Marshal. I puts on a show, mainly for his benefit, but I believe that a man has to let off a bit of steam once in a while. Dooley really loves our children and every year he dresses in those old red flannels and puts on some old fake whiskers. The youngest ones really believe in him. You should see him. He bounces the children on his knee, gives them a candy stick, and their wrapped gift. He takes great pleasure in watching their eyes light up when they open the packages. Shall I come and get him tomorrow, say, about early afternoon?"

"Tell you what Mrs. Jergens. I have to ride out your way tomorrow, you know, just making the rounds. I will bring him along with me. You don't worry yourself none. I will take good care of him."

"Thank you so much Marshal. Iffen there is any thing we can do for you, please let us know."

I saw her to the door and watched as she climbed up in that old farm wagon. Well, she was right about one thing. Dooley worked hard on that land. I knew they didn't have much, but what they had, they worked honestly for.

A crazy notion crossed my mind then. Perhaps I could add to the Jergen's family Christmas a bit. My thoughts ran wild and suddenly, a big silly mischievous grin spread slowly across my face. I looked at the small clock on the jail house wall. It was time to ride back to Laura's ranch. Tomorrow morning I would put my thoughts into action.

❖   ❖   ❖

I arrived at the ranch a little after sundown and I could feel the chill. It was getting colder. I stabled Warrior and forked some hay into both his and Mickey's feeder, then briskly walked across the yard to the main house. I could smell the stew simmering on the stove before I was half way there, and my mouth was watering. I hoped that there would be biscuits and honey to go with that stew.

Upon entering, I saw that Laura had a nice warm fire going in the main room, and I heard her moving about in the kitchen. I hung up my heavy coat and sort of carefully tiptoed to the door. Before I could peek around the corner, she said softly,

"Hello, Cole. You are just in time for supper. Anything interesting in town after I left?"

"Now just how did you know it was me?" I asked in mock surprise.

"Your spurs. You forgot to take off your spurs again. You can tiptoe all you want, but I know even the slightest sound of your spurs."

I stepped up behind her, wrapped my arms around her waist, and peered into the large pot. I was right. It was beef stew and my favorite. There was a large pan of fresh biscuits warming in the oven, as well as a pot of freshly ground dark rich coffee.

I kissed her lightly on the back of her neck and grinned as I watched the soft hairs rise slightly. She shivered a little and I watched slight goose bumps cover her arms.

"Cole Stockton, what has gotten into you? No, never mind, don't answer that. I like it."

She turned around and was suddenly in my arms. The kiss that followed was soft and warm. These were moments that I cherished most when out on some lonely trail.

Finally, we parted. "The stew is ready", she said with a warm smile, and we filled our plates.

Later, we sat together in front of the fireplace. I held her close and she laid her head on my shoulder. I watched the flickering flames lick hungrily at the logs while I silently thought to myself that this is the way that it should be always; a good woman to come home to, supper on the stove, some quiet time where a man and a woman could just sit there together reflecting upon themselves and what they meant to each other.

If I could wish for something and have it come true, I would wish for the peace of this moment for all mankind, especially at this time of year.

❦   ❦   ❦

The next day was Christmas Eve and as I thought previously, a soft white carpet covered the land. It was somewhat cloudy and cold, and I knew that there was more snow yet to come. Tonight also was the Christmas Ball in town.

After assuring Laura that I would be back in sufficient time to dress and escort her to the ball, I saddled up Warrior. I fastened my sack of plunder across the back of my saddle, put boot to stirrup and swung into the saddle. I trotted out toward town whistling a merry holiday tune to myself, grinning with the mischief that I was about to do.

Entering town, I rode straight up to the General Store and dismounted. After an hour or so, I was ready. I rode down to the jail and released Dooley, telling him to go out back and get cleaned up. I went to the livery and obtained a rental horse at no charge, telling the hostler that I had to escort a prisoner, and it being Christmas and all, the dollar fee ought to be dropped. He agreed.

Well, after another hour, Dooley and I mounted up and rode out toward his farm. He looked none the worse for wear, especially since I pumped some of J.C. Kincaid's strong coffee into him.

About an hour later, we pulled up in front of his barn. A couple of his children came out running and dancing around all excited like.

"Papa come quick, Bessie is back and she has given birth."

We dismounted and led our mounts into the barn to find Mrs. Jergens and the rest of the children gathered around the last stall. We stepped up behind the excited children and found their female sandy haired dog quietly nursing seven fat little puppies.

"Look, Mommy", said one of the little girls, "There is a puppy for each of us—and one left over".

Dooley looked at me saying, "Well, I'll be doggoned. Bessie was missing for about two weeks. We searched high and low for her, but couldn't find her. We thought that something bad must've happened to her. Looks like she purposely hid from us to have her litter."

Lorena Jergens looked up at me with appraising eyes, and suddenly I knew what Laura was getting for Christmas. I nodded my thanks, and said a silent prayer to the Almighty above for saving the day. I'd had no idea that such a simple gift was readily at hand—one that would prove etched forever in Laura's heart.

Well, after seeing that the pups and mother had a warm blanket and other necessities, we all walked over to the house. I had Dooley carry one of my sacks of plunder, and I carried the other.

I had Mrs. Jergens sit down at the kitchen table. Opening my sack I laid out a delicious apple pie, a couple of dozen fresh baked holiday cookies, and a couple of dozen fresh cinnamon rolls. The children's eyes lit up with the brilliance of a million stars on a clear night.

Taking the other sack, I reached in and handed Mrs. Jergens a bolt of flower print dress material and various other sewing notions. To each of the children, I handed a small toy, and for Dooley—I handed him a piece of paper…his account sheet from the General Store marked "PAID IN FULL". The smiles and brightly shining eyes were reward enough for the conniving mischief I had carried out.

"Merry Christmas from some good folks." I said.

Well, they wouldn't let me go until I enjoyed some of that apple pie and fresh dark coffee with them. After that, I swung up into the saddle; Dooley handed me one of the puppies, a female. Being quite cold then, with the wind picking up a mite, I took the little critter and stuffed her carefully inside my heavy winter coat. The little thing snuggled against me. It sort of tickled.

> Dooley and I shook hands. I waved to the rest of the family, turning Warrior toward Laura's ranch and briskly trotted on out. I was filled with holiday a spirit that felt good, right down to my toes. My mind and heart was sort of smiling with the deeds that I'd worked to happen. In fact, I'd say that there was a certain "glow" about me. I was happy.

A few hours later, as promised, I rode into the ranch yard, stabled Warrior and strode quite contentedly to the main house. I opened the door and there was Laura standing beside her Christmas tree. She was wearing a most beautiful full-length gown of deep blue. Her dark hair lay softly down over her shoulders and a matching blue ribbon held an ivory broach at her throat. Her eyes were shining with excitement. To put it straight, she was simply breathtaking.

Laura smiled broadly as I stood there just looking at her with deep appreciation. A sudden gleam of pleasure flashed across her crystal blue eyes, and she handed me my gift.

"Hurry! Open it. I wanted you to have this before we went to the ball."

I kind've took my time slowly opening the small package while she fidgeted and danced around all excited like.

Finally, I removed the top of the box, and my heart thumped some. It was the most beautiful watch and chain a man could ask for. It even had my initials, R.C.S., engraved on the casing. I was speechless.

Laura came up to me, and put her arms around me. That's when she felt the small bulge wiggling inside my coat. She stepped back and looked questioningly at me. A quiet little whimper caused her eyes to widen and suddenly a furry little face peered out of my coat.

"Merry Christmas", I said softly. I held my breath waiting for Laura's reaction. She shook her head a bit, smiled, and then looked deep into my eyes. It was a soft and tender look, almost like a mother would give a newborn child.

She stepped forward again, and took the furry little critter in her arms. She cuddled it to her cheek. I could see that it was love at first sight.

I know that I must have flushed at that moment, for I felt my own cheeks grow warm. Laura stepped back to me then and with one arm around me, gave me a soft kiss, followed with an almost audible "Thank you". I could see the soft mist in her eyes. She was happy.

Laura set about fixing a place for her new puppy while I shaved and changed clothes. This was her night, and I wanted to make it most wonderful for her. I proudly positioned my new gold watch and chain on my vest.

As a passing comment, Laura said, "Those wranglers sure ate a lot of baked goods today. I could have sworn that I made more than enough, but somehow it seemed to have been less than previous times."

A sheepish grin spread slowly across my face and I had to turn away to keep from laughing. Well, they went to good use. There is nothing more heart-warming than watching a small child munch a fresh baked cookie.

We drove to town in the buckboard. You could see the lights of celebration from miles away. The main street had lanterns lit all along it, and from the town hall there was music—happy music. I helped Laura down from the wagon, and we walked arm in arm to the door.

Once inside, I abided by her wishes and checked my gunbelt at the door. My second Colt was safely tucked inside my belt under my suit coat. Somehow I got the feeling that she knew it, but accepted it.

The small orchestra began one of Laura's favorite ballads. We walked hand in hand to the center of the dance floor. Turning toward each other, our eyes met, and once again the smoldering passion lit the fires of our souls. We were oblivious to everyone else in the room as we slowly stepped out in time with the music. We looked lovingly into each other's eyes and unto each other a silent promise was made.

Tonight I was at peace with myself and the world seemed at peace with itself, and that is what Christmas is all about.

"THE GREATEST GIFT"

Laura Sumner placed the last ornament on the Douglas fir standing in the corner of her living room. She then stepped back a few steps and scrutinized the entire Christmas tree. Yes—that was it. It was a most beautiful tree.

Every year on the Sumner Horse Ranch, it was custom for Laura's Boys, her wranglers, to ride to the foothills of the Colorado Rocky Mountains and select the festive tree for their most beloved Boss Wrangler. Each year they selected an eight to ten foot, full-bodied tree for Laura.

Although the boys set the tree in a stout stand, Laura always performed the decoration ceremony herself. This year was no exception. She looked thoughtfully at the decorated tree and smiled. She always loved this time of year. She thought to herself,

"The boys have outdone themselves this year. Cole will just love this tree. And—he is going to love the gift that I got him."

She thought more, "Thinking of Cole, I wonder just where he is. I haven't heard from him in days. He is escorting those two prisoners to Judge Wilkerson's Court from Cheyenne, Wyoming, and he is supposed to be back here by tomorrow. Oh well, maybe he didn't have time to wire his departure."

🍁   🍁   🍁

I had dropped off two murderous men for trial at Judge Wilkerson's court and was on my way back to Laura's ranch. In fact, Warrior and I were just about thirty to thirty-five miles from the edge of Laura's land. I had bought her a most beautiful pair of silver spurs for a gift and was lost in thoughts about it.

The weather was deathly cold and I was bundled up in my heaviest winter coat. Warrior was taking the trip well but winter has its own way of making man and animal thirsty, so we sort of drifted down into the riverbed that we were paralleling.

We had just rounded a jagged rock formation when the terrifying scream seared through our ears. Warrior reared suddenly, his front hooves pawing the air. My hand instinctively went for the Colt in the belt behind my back as I jerked my head toward the left.

The yellowish flash sailed right at me and before I could react, the cougar hit me with his entire weight and I was summarily thrown from the saddle to hit the frozen ground. The Colt flew from my hand and as the heavy cat's fangs gnashed at me, I threw up my left arm to shield myself and then pain seared into my forearm as the steel like jaws clamped around the flesh of my arm. I could feel the warm wetness of my own blood running free.

Warrior screamed and reared. Suddenly, the cat's attention turned to him and I rolled away scrambling to find my Colt.

Horse and cat faced each other with deadly intent. The cougar crouched, muscles coiling for a powerful spring. Warrior was rearing and kicking out, front hooves pawing the air ready to stomp the life out of this dangerous adversary.

The cat circled warily, then suddenly leaped and landed square on Warrior's back, clinging to the saddle. Warrior was screaming, rearing and bucking wildly in an effort to shake the big cat off.

I found my Colt and turned once more to face the big cat. Warrior's saddle suddenly slipped to the left side with the heavy weight and the cat lost his grip, tumbling to the frozen earth. I fired. My round smacked into the cats shoulder area; yet, even though wounded he lunged at me.

I stepped backward a step as the huge cougar leaped right at me and then, the next thing I knew, we were both slamming into the icy river.

The cat clawed at me with death in his yellow eyes as the swiftness of the current dragged both of us down stream. I struggled to hold the powerful jaws away from me as the strong current began pulling us both under the water and faster downstream. I took deep breaths as we bobbed up and down in the water.

Suddenly, the cat turned loose of me and began fighting for his life in the now raging white-water current. We drifted neck deep only a few yards apart when the current surged faster. The cat clawed water desperately trying to make it to the left shoreline.

I could make out the roar of thunder in the immediate distance and knew that a tremendous waterfall lay up ahead. I also tried to swim toward the opposite shoreline, but my heavy water logged coat was dragging me with the current. I was exhausted from fighting off the big cat. I closed my eyes and thought of Laura.

Suddenly, both the cat and I were sailing out in mid-air. I fell and heard my own voice yelling. The cat screamed wretchedly. I saw it hit the rocky cliff below, bounce, and then slip limp and silent into the deadly current just as I hit the raging water myself.

I suddenly hit into the rock-bottomed water below and something smashed against my head. Instant nausea shot through my body and I fought to keep consciousness. Blood oozed down into my eyes as I grabbed wildly at a large root protruding from the embankment along the shore. I vaguely recalled what I was doing as I pulled myself up onto it before I passed out from the pain.

The dark chestnut felt the weight of the huge cat on his back and began to fiercely buck and kick. Suddenly the saddle slipped down his side and the heavy weight fell off of him. He turned hard and kicked out, narrowly missing the cougar's head.

The large cat had momentarily turned his attention back to Cole Stockton. He crouched, showing his deadly fangs, then suddenly leaped at the man.

Warrior rushed forward too late and watched helplessly as both man and cougar splashed into the icy waters of the river. Warrior tried to follow into the water, but the current was too strong. He turned and floundered back to the shore and stood there, saddle hanging down his side and shaking with the cold.

The dark chestnut turned once again to the river but man and the beast were out of sight. The wildly raging river had seemingly swallowed them up. He turned and slowly began the journey back to the Sumner Horse Ranch by his himself—reins trailing. Darkness was falling and in the distance, Warrior heard the lonely moaning howl of the timber wolf. Night fell across the Lower Colorado landscape and the bitter cold sifted in from the North.

Laura Sumner finished washing and putting away her supper dishes, then sat in on the sofa in front of her fireplace along with Lady, her blonde haired dog. She watched the dancing flames consume the heavy winter logs and thought of Cole Stockton. She smiled a bit at the reflection, and then a sudden foreboding shudder rippled through her body.

Visions of frozen wasteland and death surged across her mind. She shivered with the thoughts and held her arms about herself as she mouthed the words describing what she felt, "Cole! Cole is in danger!"

She rose from the sofa to peer out the window. A silvery moon glistened on the white carpet of snow outside her home. There was nothing she could do at this point. She could only think about Cole and where he might be. There came a sudden shudder. What danger might have befallen him?

It was near to midnight when Laura, exhausted and worried, moved into her bedroom, slipped into her heavy woolen nightgown and settled into bed. She slept fitfully, turning here and there—wakening several times to search the darkness with swollen, watery eyes and wishing that Cole Stockton was safely back at her ranch.

Warrior trudged slowly toward the Southeast—heading for home and his warm stall. Night had fallen; yet, he picked his way along the rocky ground, ever in the same direction. Periodically, he stopped and sniffed the crisp air. The scent in the wind was unmistakable. He was being trailed; rather, he was being stalked. Soon, they would be on his trail and they would be coming fast for him.

The dark chestnut moved quicker this time. He knew the danger that lurked shortly behind him and also that within moments he would have to run for his life.

Suddenly, loud howls and snarls sounded within fifty yards of the stallion. He immediately bolted into a gallop, then into a stretched out run. Down the slope of the mountainside he ran, through the tree line of pine and aspen racing for the bottom and open area. Howls and hungry snarls beared down on him. The wolves were gaining ground in their hunger for his flesh.

Momentarily, the forest gave way to a long meadow. Warrior gained a second wind and now he was stretched out running for his life. The wolves were spread out behind him, denying him to turn least he be flanked. They were running hard—tongues hanging out, as they could almost taste the hot flesh of this dark chestnut. Warrior was tiring. Soon the entire pack would be on him, dragging him down for the kill.

Suddenly, a river appeared before him and he surged forward at breakneck speed. He reached the edge of the embankment and with a powerful lunge, sailed across the twenty-three foot space, landing with a thud near the other bank.

Warrior's powerful hind legs scrambled, slipping in the muddy earth for several long moments, as the wolves entered the icy water. They were swimming toward him.

The dark chestnut dug his rear hooves in and up and over the embankment he went—almost stumbling, yet somehow keeping his footing. He broke again into a steady gallop, putting distance between himself and his natural foes.

Warrior had gone but fifty yards when shots rang out behind him. He strained his ears, but heard nothing more of the long low moan of the carnivorous animals behind him. He slowed to a steady walk—always to the Southeast.

Seth Williams was out from his cabin following a deer trail when he heard the melee coming toward him. He hunkered down along the embankment of the wild river and waited.

Suddenly, a heavily lathered, but nonetheless magnificent, chestnut stallion appeared. The animal was running all out with a saddle slapping against his side with reins trailing. Right on his heels was a pack of wild hungry timber wolves, snapping and yelping in their frenzy to run down this gallant steed.

Seth held his Winchester at the ready as he watched the horse sail across the embankment and labor up the closest side. He grinned hard as the frenzied wolves entered the water, swimming to their prey. Wolf pelts brought good bounty money and Seth was needy of the cash. He whipped the rifle to his shoulder and began to methodically earn his dues.

How long I lay on that frozen root I don't know. I only knew that I was cold—down to the bone cold and frosted over. I shook my head to regain my senses, and it hurt something fierce. I touched my hand to my icy forehead to find it caked with dried blood. My left arm also ached with dull pain.

I thought hard. I couldn't seem to remember what had happened or how I came to lie on that root along the riverbed. I searched my mind more. I suddenly realized that I couldn't even remember my name. "Who am I? What am I doing here?"

Something nagged at the back of my memory though, and that nagging thought told me that I was in danger and that above all else, I had to find shelter and warmth in a hurry. I crawled slowly up the large root to the embankment and then labored up and over it to lay exhausted in tall frozen grass for a long minute or so to catch my breath. I thought also then that,

"Not only do I not know who or what I am, I don't even know where I am."

I only knew that I was icy chilled right down to my bones and that my fingers and toes were numb with cold. I had to think hard. "What should I do?"

The thought that I was near to frost bit suddenly streaked across my mind and just as suddenly; I knew what I had to do.

I pried myself out of that icy frozen heavy coat and while shivering, took handfuls of snow and rubbed it all over my face and hands. Somehow I recalled that was a method of treating frostbite. It hurt like hell, but I kept rubbing snow all over me and after a while, I could feel some circulation back in my numbed fingers and face. I had to think more. Where could I find shelter from this freezing cold? Darkness was coming and I felt the wind pick up a bit. It would get colder. I had to find a place to somehow get a fire started.

Even as I stood shivering, I slowly looked down at my waist. I was wearing a gun belt and sitting in the holster with a thong over the hammer was a Colt Revolver. I touched the butt of it and my thumb flipped the rawhide thong off of the hammer. I drew it and looked at it carefully. It was well cared for and on the walnut grips there was carved the initials "RCS". Now what did that stand for? I had no idea.

I holstered the revolver and looked around. There seemed to be a heavy thicket close to some rocks in the distance. I surmised that the rocks would afford some type of shelter for me.

I bent down painfully and picked up the heavy frozen coat and dragged it with me. If, I thought, I could somehow get a fire going, I could thaw out this coat and then, maybe be warm. I had to try, but first I had to reach those rocks up ahead. Shivering, I trudged slowly, painfully, all the way to the rock formation.

It may have taken only thirty minutes or so to reach them rocks, but it seemed like an eternity. Once there, I picked my way through some heavy frozen brush and suddenly, I found a hole in the rocks. I made my way cautiously into it.

It turned out to be somewhat of a half cave. It was shelter enough from the wind. But, I still needed warmth and that meant a fire.

I thought hard to clear my mind from thoughts of just lying down and going to sleep. I was exhausted, but a nagging thought told me that if I closed my eyes at this point that I would never wake up—I would die here in this frozen wilderness.

I sat down to rest a bit in that hole in the rocks and as I slowly looked around, it came to me. There were dried leaves and dried grass along the edge of the cave and there were a bit larger twigs and such just outside. My mind began churning with all kinds of thoughts.

What if I built a fire? How would I light it? How much tinder and wood would I need? Is there enough to last the night?

Those were the thoughts that crossed my otherwise blank mind. Well, I would build that fire. I got to my hands and knees and scraped out a dirt ring about two feet all around. Then, with pain filled hands and fingers, I pulled up bunches of dried grass and gathered up dried leaves. I piled them together.

Well, it looked like a fire—but I still needed some good wood, just in case I figured out how to light it. It took me the next hour to gather up what I figured was enough wood to last for a while. Then, I sat down and just looked at that pile of tinder and sticks.

I reached to that heavy ice covered coat and began rummaging through the pockets. Something stabbed my frozen fingers and I quickly withdrew my hand from the inside pocket. I carefully pried the pocket open and peered inside. It appeared that there was a piece of shiny metal in there.

Again, I reached into that pocket, as carefully as I could. I grasped the metal thing with numbed fingers and withdrew it. It was a **Silver Star** engraved with the words, "United States Marshal."

Something in the recesses of my mind made sense. I was a lawman. But still, I didn't know who I was or where I was. I sighed. At least some things appeared to come back to me.

In the left side pocket, I found a jackknife, a pack of cigarette papers, a small sack of tobacco, and two matches. I appeared to be in luck. I painfully made my way to my fire. I held one of the matches in my numbed fingers. I closed my eyes hard for a long moment and prayed that it would light. I struck the match on a rock.

Again and again, I struck the match against the rock. It was too wet. It would not light. I must save the other until it dried out. But, could I wait that long? How long would it take?

No. I needed that fire now!

My attention was suddenly diverted once again to the revolver at my side. A thought suddenly hit me. If I fired that Colt, there would be a flame from the barrel. I had to try it. I reached to my belt and withdrew the Colt. I cocked it and laid the barrel close to that tinder. I squeezed the trigger.

"Click"

I sighed a heavy sigh. Everything seemed against me. The cartridges were wet and needed drying out also. I tried it again.

"Click" and again, "Click"

I hung my head and said unto myself a silent prayer. I swallowed hard and my throat hurt from the dryness. Not only was I cold to the bone, near frozen, I was dry inside. I had to try once more. I cocked back that hammer and held it again to the tinder.

The shot that split the air rang in my near frozen ears for several minutes, but flame shot from the muzzle and the tinder burst alive with fingers of flame. I shivered with excitement as I lay the Colt to one side to began feeding sticks into the small fire.

After a half-hour or so, I felt warmth coming back into my body. I lay that frozen coat next to the fire and within a few minutes I could see steam rising from it. I felt it and it was warm. It was drying out. It would take time, but time was what I had—I had a lot of time to get that coat dry as well as the rest of the cartridges in my gunbelt.

Finally, I felt warm enough to sleep. I pulled a couple of good-sized pieces of dry tree trunk into the fire and leaned back against the rocky wall of the small cave. I watched as those pieces also caught up in the flames and I began to breathe a lot easier. It was time to rest.

I closed my eyes and suddenly, a young dark haired woman appeared. She looked like she was missing someone. Who? Could it be me? Who was she? Who was I?

I lay down somewhat next to the fire and within minutes, slipped into a deep sleep. The dreams began then.

I dreamed of a beautiful valley surrounded by mountains and in that valley was a horse ranch. I could just about make out the lay of that ranch when I thought that I heard someone calling out a name. I felt myself holding my breath.

In my dreams, a beautiful young dark haired woman stepped out to the porch of a ranch house and she seemed to be calling out a name. I listened intently, and I could see her calling, but the name just would not come to me. I slipped deeper into a dead sleep for I was exhausted.

❦   ❦   ❦

It was the next day at around five o'clock in the evening, that Judd Ellison, Juan Soccorro, and Eli Johnson heard the whinny and the three of them looked to the gates of the Sumner Horse Ranch.

"My God", breathed Jud Ellison, "it's Warrior. Look at him, he's a mess. Where is Cole?"

Warrior slowly walked, head drooping, almost staggering through the gates of the Sumner Ranch and headed for the stables. The saddle was now hanging below his belly and he looked ragged and muddy. Dried streaks of blood were caked on his back and shoulders.

Juan Soccorro slowly approached the dark chestnut with soothing words. Warrior stopped in his tracks and turned to look at Juan. He shied away a few steps, but Juan kept moving toward him—always with soft words. Judd Ellison turned to Eli Johnson,

"Eli, get over to the main house and you tell Miss Laura. You tell her that she has got to be here right now."

Eli Johnson backed slowly away from the scene, and then, dashed to the house. He knocked excitedly on the door—continuously until it opened. Laura eyed him questioningly. Then, as he mentioned "Warrior", her eyes lit up and she shoved past him to run toward the stables. Eli was right on her heels.

Laura stopped suddenly as she took in Warrior. The horse looked terrible and wild-eyed. He wouldn't let anyone near him. Laura swallowed hard and then moved slowly one step at a time toward him. She spoke soothingly to him and held out her hand to him. Juan moved out of her way. This was a job for Laura.

Long minutes ticked by, but Laura was patient. Finally, Warrior hung his head a bit and moved toward her. Tears suddenly rolled out of Laura's eyes as she saw the condition of the horse.

Warrior was then nuzzling Laura's shoulder as if to say "I know you and I am glad to be home."

Laura held the horse's head to her shoulder and with cracked voice looked at Juan.

"Get the saddle off of him Juan. Be very gentle. He is hurt and afraid. God, what has happened to Cole? He wouldn't leave Warrior like this. Something dreadfully wrong has happened to him."

Juan Soccorro stripped the saddle and trappings off of Warrior and then Laura led him into his stall. She filled his feeder with fresh hay and two hands full of oats. She tenderly began the task of examining the wounds in an effort to understand what happened to the horse.

Suddenly, she turned and moved to the stable entrance where Judd and all the boys stood quietly watching her. She almost whispered,

"Judd, there are claw marks all over Warrior's back and shoulders. He was attacked by a large cat—possibly a cougar. It's too late right now, but at sunup I want every wrangler in the saddle. We are riding north and backtracking Warrior. I believe that Cole is alive but hurt. In any case, he is in danger. We are going to find him."

Judd Ellison looked deeply into Laura's eyes. He saw the pain and the worry.

"Don't worry Miss Laura. Cole's a tough man. He knows the wilds and he knows how to survive. We will find him."

Judd saw the mist in her eyes as she nodded, then turned and walked slowly back to the house. Juan moved to Warrior's side and began to apply salve to the wounds. He rubbed the animal down as best as possible and spoke softly to him,

"Warrior, you know what happened. Please tell Juan what you know—for Miss Laura."

❧   ❧   ❧

Laura closed the door to her house. Then, she stood for a long minute, back against the door and head lowered in thought. Tears rolled down her strained face.

"Oh, Cole. Are you really alive? I have to know. I have to find you and know for myself. Please tell me where you are."

Darkness came and Laura moved to her room. She dressed in her warm flannel gown and blew out the oil lamp. She lay there in the darkness thinking about Cole Stockton. She closed her eyes and thought hard. She whispered his name.

Slowly the vision came to her. She saw a darkened shadow of a man wandering the wilds with no direction. Snow was abundant. He was cold, feverish, and hungry. He was hurt and bleeding. The man walked aimlessly without purpose. Danger lurked all around him.

Then, as suddenly as the vision appeared, a veil of darkness fell over the man and the vision was gone. Laura trembled in the darkness and swore softly to herself. "As I live and breathe, Cole Stockton, I will find you, no matter what. I know that you are alive and no one can tell me different. Always know Cole that I love you and I am coming for you. Never give up, Cole, I **will** find you."

Laura turned over on her side, snuggling to her pillows. Softly she whispered his name again before drifting into fitful slumber.

❦   ❦   ❦

Daylight came and it was still cold. I put some more wood on the fire, watching it blaze up. The ensuing warmth felt real good. My head ached with a dull throbbing pain and it was very tender along my forehead. In fact, there was a swollen gash that I hadn't realized before. I thought then that I must've really been whacked with something.

Still, I could not remember a thing about how it happened, nor who I was. Well, I would sit here to think for a while longer. I had the distinct notion that I should be heading somewhere, but for the life of me, I couldn't remember where.

I was alone. I had no horse, no hat, no food—well, maybe, and I once again searched the pockets of that heavy coat. It was dry now and in the right hand pocket, I found a small packet of beef trail jerky. I was in luck.

I sat there, ripping off a good size piece of jerky with my teeth. It sure tasted good. I chewed it slowly, savoring each moment of it. I thought whilst I chewed and soon realized that I couldn't stay here. I had to travel. I was supposed to be somewhere. I just wish that I could remember where.

It was, I reckon, around early morning when I crawled out of that small crevice that I called a cave and took stock of my bearings. I noted the direction of the sun and knew that I was somewhere in the West—but where in the West?

Something flashed across my mind then that said to travel south.

I nodded to myself. Well, it was as good a direction as any to travel. I watched the position of the sun as I began walking in a southerly direction. The air was crisp and cold as I walked slowly, always watching for something. What it was, I didn't know, but something told me to be very wary.

I had gone but a few miles when I heard sounds. I closed my eyes, and could envision horses. Somebody was riding a horse in my direction. I caught the general direction and watched very carefully. A few minutes passed, and then, I drove myself to the snow covered frozen ground.

A group of about five or six wildly dressed Indians moved into sight from some trees not a hundred yards down slope from my right front. They moved silently, talking amongst themselves with sign.

Something told me that this was no hunting party. This was a group of warriors who rode with deadly intent. I hugged the cold ground and watched them while they moved onward toward the South—the same direction that I was headed.

I waited a good half-hour or so after they passed before I moved. I wanted a good distance between them and me. Finally, I rose to my knees. Lying in that snow chilled me once again, but in thinking about it, I would rather be chilled, than dead.

I decided to travel parallel to those warriors. I didn't want to suddenly come up on one while trudging absentmindedly through the snow.

Well, I had it to do. I knew that I was a lawman and that I was supposed to be somewhere. The fact that I had no horse and no hat, but still carried a weapon led me to believe that perhaps I had been waylaid and left for dead. Well, I would show them. I would make it to whatever lay south of this wilderness.

I started walking again. I walked for an hour, rested for a half-hour, walked for an hour and so on until I had gone for about half a day.

The pit of my stomach felt weak and nauseous. My head still throbbed with pain and once or twice, I had to just sit down there in the snow and hang my head for a while. I was hungry and it was showing. I needed to think about something to eat for nourishment. The beef trail jerky had been my first meal in God knows when and I'd eaten it all. Now, I must find something.

It was right about that time that gunfire erupted in the distance. It lasted only about a quarter of an hour and then, all was silent. I watched the sky carefully as black smoke drifted up through the pines in the distance. Someone had been attacked by the warrior party ahead of me. I could almost feel the outcome. Why did they always have to burn everything?

Well, there was nothing I could do for whomever it was, except maybe bury them. I would give them warriors a long hour to complete their tasks of misery, then, I would trudge my way to the scene and do what needed to be done. In the meantime, I just lay down on that cold ground and waited.

I gave them almost two hours before I rose and stomped life back into my toes. There wasn't more than a couple of hours of daylight left and I wanted to get to the scene as quickly as possible. I began trudging my way to where I had seen that smoke billowing up.

Two hours later I knew that I was close. I could smell the burnt wood. I followed the scent and it got stronger by the minute. It wasn't long before I found the small clearing.

It was as I suspected. A small cabin lay in smoldering ashes, burnt to the ground. There were two bodies. Both men by their looks were prospectors. The warriors had stripped them of all before shooting their bodies full of arrows. Any stock that they had was long gone with the raiding party.

I decided to look around in hopes of finding at least a forgotten tin of food. I was in luck. I found two tins of beans.

Well, first things first. I was sorely in need of nourishment. I sat down near the still smoldering pile of ashes. There was a kind of warmth coming from it.

I shakily took out that jackknife I found in the coat pocket and jammed it into one of the cans. I worked the blade fervently and finally had an open can. I looked over at the two deceased and whispered a silent "Thank you." Well, them beans tasted mighty good.

Later, I found a half-burned shovel and commenced to dig what I could of a couple of graves. They would have to do.

After that was done, I said a silent prayer for both men and then, I looked for a warm place for the night. Them coals still smoldered warmly, so I lay down right close to them and took stock of myself.

I still couldn't remember who I was or what had happened to me, but I did know that I was a lawman, and that I had me a Colt Revolver with five rounds in the cylinder with about twenty cartridges within the loops of my gunbelt. They would have to do.

I had one can of beans, a jackknife, and a heavy coat. That was about it. I shore wished I could find a horse somewhere. But even with a mount, where would I ride? I didn't know. Well, I needed rest, so I lay back and closed my eyes. Sleep came quickly.

Laura Sumner was awake before the sun came up. She fumbled for a match at her nightstand and finding one, struck it. She lit the oil lamp at her bedside, then lay there for a long moment. She thought of her quest on this morn. Cole

Stockton was missing in the wilds of the Lower Colorado. She had the distinct feeling that he was alive, but hurt in some way. She was going to take her boys and find him if it was the last thing she ever did.

Laura slid out of bed and shucked her flannel nightgown. She grabbed up her Levi's, pulling them on. She got out her warmest winter shirt to slip into it. Next, she pulled her boots on and rising from the bed, stomped them in place.

Lady slid from under the bed and looked at Laura with sad eyes. It was as if the dog knew exactly what was on Laura's mind, feeling her sadness. Laura forced a smile, speaking softly to the yellow haired dog "I know, Lady. You miss him too. Don't worry, we will find him and bring him home."

Laura turned, and with Lady at her heels, went through the large living room. She didn't even stop at the kitchen to make coffee. She grabbed up her gunbelt, strapped it on, reached for her chaps and strode out the door toward the Wrangler's Cook Shack. A light shined in the windows. The boys were already up also and grabbing a bite to eat and some coffee.

Laura opened the door to find all of the Sumner Horse Ranch wranglers ready for the trail as they sipped up black coffee and ate a breakfast of eggs, steak, and potatoes. They all looked up as Laura entered.

Judd looked deep into Laura's eyes and then silently nodded. "Come, Miss Laura. Have some breakfast and coffee with us."

Laura nodded back as she sat down with her boys. They felt her concern. Deep down, all of Laura's boys thought the same. One of their friends was in trouble and they would ride to hell and back to help.

The sun was just peeking over the closest rim in the East when Laura Sumner and ten riders swung into the saddle and pointed their mounts toward the North. Each carried the tools of survival and a good bait of forage for their mounts. This might take days.

They followed Warrior's tracks as much as possible and slowly the story began to unfold. Warrior was walking slow and had stumbled and fell several times during the last miles to the ranch. But, he always managed to get up and trek onward toward his stall. He held a purpose in his mind and that purpose was to get home.

The first day on the trail came and went with no sign of Cole Stockton. The Sumner Ranch group made camp and Laura had them build the fire high so as to be seen from miles around.

"I don't care if renegades see it", she said straight out, "Let them come. There are enough of us to handle it. I want a fire that will show in the night—a beacon so to speak."

All of the wranglers knew exactly what she was speaking of and they would be ready for anything. They would be taking chances not normally taken in the wilds.

Laura hunkered down by the fire with her boys. They sipped on cups of hot coffee and ate a hot meal of beans, thick sliced bacon, biscuits, and some of the steak strips left over from their breakfast. Laura spoke to her boys as they sat around the fire.

"Boys, I don't know exactly what we are riding into. I only know that Cole is out here somewhere and that he is hurt and alone. You all saw Warrior come in alone and he looked a fright. I don't care how long it takes, I don't care what it takes—I want to find Cole."

Laura then lowered her eyes and head for a long moment. She continued, "If any of you want to turn back now for any reason, tell me. I for one have got to continue. I must know, one way or another, just what happened and I will not rest until I know the truth."

One by one, all of Laura's wranglers nodded to her silently. Each knew what their chances were. But, Laura was their Boss Wrangler, and where Laura went, they went. They all settled down for the night.

Laura slipped into her blankets and closed her eyes. "Cole, please hear me. We are coming to you. Don't ever give up."

And then, Laura slipped into a worried sleep.

Eli Johnson and Mike Wilkes drew the first watch of the night. They each thought of Cole in their own way as they stood guard on the Wrangler camp. Each in his own way, wished that Cole would see the fire and work his way toward them.

I woke with a morning chill in my bones. The smoldering ashes of the burned out cabin died around early morning. I sat up, feeling bone tired. I ached all over. My breathing was heavy and all of a sudden, I coughed. It was a cough deep in my chest and I knew that I was getting sick from the constant cold. My voice was also somewhat hoarse and I felt warm. I was feverish.

Even so, I had to move as long as I could. I had to try and find someplace or someone to help me. Slowly, I gathered my meager items of survival around me. I tried to stand up, but faltered. I crumbled to my hands and knees and suddenly, I wanted to retch out my insides. I did just that.

I felt very weak and wanted to just lay down in the snow and rest. Suddenly, a distant voice in my mind told me to get up and keep moving. It was a softly spoken woman's voice. I listened carefully to my mind. I had heard that voice before—always in the back of my mind.

The vision of a dark haired, blue eyed woman entered my mind for just a split second—and then it was gone. I didn't know who she was, but she was calling me and I felt that I had to go to her.

With all my strength, I lifted myself up and with one foot in front of the other; I started south once again. How long I walked, I didn't know, but somewhere all of a sudden; I smelled a campfire. I stopped and shook my head in an effort to regain some good sense.

I had to be cautious. And that is the way that I half stumbled and half-walked toward the increasing odor of wood smoke. My hand involuntarily reached down and touched the butt of the Colt at my side. Somehow, it seemed natural to me.

Long minutes later, I approached what seemed to be a small camp within a stand of pines. It appeared to be somewhat hidden and had I not smelled of it first, I never would have seen it.

I slowly made my way toward it and then, I could smell horses. These people whoever they were, had horses. I closed my eyes for a long moment. A slight vision of a dark colored horse filtered through my mind and then faded. I stepped closer to this camp.

Now, I could make out three rough looking men sitting by a fire and drinking what appeared to be coffee. It was coffee. I could smell it. I swallowed hard, and it hurt. I was drying out inside. I had to have water at least, but a good cup of coffee seemed like only a hand's length away.

I stepped to the edge of a small clearing and faced the three men. I took a deep breath and with forced voice, said, "Hallo the camp! I need help and that coffee smells real good."

Well, the three of them looked up at me as one and their faces turned white as a sheet. Something in the back of my mind told me that I was about to die. All three men jumped up and went for their guns. They snarled obscenities at me and my own hand instinctively swept to the Colt at my side. In the next instant I was firing into them. I heard the whistle of hot lead as it sailed past me and thunked into trees behind me.

The one thing that bothered me most was that those horses all reared and bucked against their makeshift "picket" line when the shooting started. When it finished, there wasn't a horse left. They all shied out and went a running for parts unknown.

Thirty seconds, I figure, and I once again stood alone. All three men were dead. Well, I knew a bit more about myself now. I was a lawman, a fast gun, and there were men that despised me—enough to jump up and immediately draw weapons. I wondered about these men while I emptied my cylinder of spent cartridges and reaching to my belt, slipped in fresh ones. It seemed like the thing to do.

Well, fact was, that there was some coffee left. I reached down with shaking hands and weak knees to a cup and that pot. There was also some bacon and beans in a pan on the side of the fire. They wouldn't need them anymore. I ate their breakfast and drank up their coffee.

I didn't have a shovel or anything to dig a grave with, so I left them as they lay and started once more toward the South. I was beginning to shiver with fever now, but at least I was fed and had a bit of hot coffee to somewhat sustain me. I kept on trudging toward my destination—the South and whatever lay before me.

Laura Sumner and her wranglers continued to follow the sometimes-faint trail left by Warrior. The wind and occasional snow flurries periodically brushed out the tracks. Laura's boys were used to tracking wild horses and bit by bit, if they lost the trail, they re-found it.

Finally, around early afternoon on the second day, they came across a small cabin. The cabin had ten fresh wolf pelts nailed to the walls. A thin trail of smoke came from the makeshift chimney and the wrangler bunch rode slowly up to it, Winchesters peaceably cradled in their arms.

Seth Williams was boiling himself a small pot of coffee when he heard the unmistakable sound of a lot of horses outside his cabin. He turned from his small fireplace and taking up his Winchester, moved to the door to crack it a bit and peer out.

Before his cabin was a group of eleven riders. All had Winchesters ready and they looked wary. They seemed to be led by a woman—a right pretty woman with dark hair and crystal blue eyes. She wore trail clothes just like a man, and resting on her hip was a Colt Lightning Revolver. She looked to know how to use it.

Seth opened the door of his cabin and stepped out to face the visitors. The woman looked deep into Seth's eyes before speaking.

"Mr., I'm sorry to bother you, but, we're back trailing a horse from our ranch. A dark chestnut with one white stocking and lighter colored mane and tail. It could possibly have had a saddle slipping down its side. Did you happen see such an animal in the past few days?"

Seth Williams looked up at the woman and grinned a bit. He nodded affirmatively.

"Yes Ma'am, I did. About three days ago it was. I was just out to the river looking for game when I heard a commotion and out of the tree line from the other side of the river comes this wild-eyed fine looking chestnut with saddle flapping on his left side. Right on his heels were a pack of timber wolves. Them's the ones nailed to my walls."

"Did you think to back track the horse?"

"Yes. I did backtrack for a few miles and then the tracks were wiped out by the quick snow blizzard that rushed in on me. I had no chance to continue, but only make it back to this here cabin just in time. It was freezing cold out there—not fit for man nor beast."

Judd Ellison spoke up. "Thank you Mr.?"

"Name's Seth—Seth Williams."

"Thank you very much Mr. Williams for the information. We will be going now, but is there anything that we can do for you? Perhaps a bit of tobacco or some coffee, beans or sugar?"

Seth's eyes lit up at the sound of "sugar". He hadn't had any sugar with his coffee in a coon's age.

The Sumner Ranch bunch left Seth Williams with a pound of sugar, a pound of coffee beans, some bacon, and three large cans of beans. Seth marveled at the hospitality of this bunch. To him, he had only mentioned that he had seen this animal. To the Sumner Ranch wranglers, Seth had not only seen Warrior but also saved his life.

They turned and rode directly to the river. The Wranglers looked up and down the river embankment and suddenly, Mike Wilkes shouted out, "Well, I'll be damned. Come here and look at this!"

Laura and the others rode immediately to him.

"Miss Laura! Look here. See those deep marks in the mud there? A horse was here. See those marks? A horse landed right here in the mud and with those outer marks, it was scrambling like the devil hisself was on its heels. God,

Miss Laura—look at the distance from that opposite embankment. That's got to be at least twenty-five feet."

Laura looked at the distance and tears came to her eyes. Warrior was chased by wolves and in desperation jumped across the river embankment—almost twenty-five feet to escape death. He barely made it, but with sheer determination, scrambled up and over the embankment to safety.

She swallowed hard. They still hadn't found the point where Cole and Warrior had separated. Laura turned to her wranglers and said, "I feel that we are very close to the truth now. Let's go across the river and find him."

Without another word, Laura heeled Mickey into the cold waters of the river toward the opposite bank. Laura's wranglers, without hesitation, rode directly into the stream. Nearing the embankment, Laura glanced back. All were with her.

❧   ❧   ❧

A man afoot in the wilds travels mighty slow. There is thick brush, heavy stands of pine and aspen, steep hills, rocky crevices, deep chasms, and wild animals. Danger lurks everywhere.

I moved the best that I could and by now, my boots felt heavy on my feet. I could feel the fever taking toll on my body. My mind was sometimes confused. Still, I wandered to what I believed to be ever South in direction.

More and more, my head ached causing me to take more frequent stops to rest. My breathing was laborious. The bitter cold didn't help either. The further I traveled, the more tired I became. I was half walking, half stumbling along a slight ridge and thinking—trying to think straight—trying to piece myself together.

The vision of that woman was on my mind. She appeared to be telling me something. The more I thought about her, the more she seemed familiar to me. But, I just couldn't put my finger on it. She was elusive, yet hung there in my mind and wouldn't let go.

I must have been deep in thought, because I didn't see the crevice in front of me. Suddenly, I stepped out with my right foot and there was nothing there. I immediately fell to my thigh in a large hole. Damn! It hurt! I just sat there gritting my teeth and swearing a blue streak.

Now, I wondered if my leg was broken. That was all that I'd need now. It sure felt like it. I grimaced and lay back a bit, one foot was underneath me and the other, inside a crevice.

I let out a long pain filled sigh and closed my eyes. I could see bright lights and stars shooting inside my head. Slowly, ever so slowly, I leaned to the left and began the painful process of pulling my leg out of the crevice. It hurt with every inch.

Finally after what seemed an eternity, I dislodged my leg and lay back in the snow to catch my breath. It hurt like hell.

Long minutes later, I rose with considerable effort and slowly worked my right boot off. My ankle and lower leg were swollen, but I couldn't find any break in the bones. I was lucky? It seemed like I had only managed a severe sprain of my lower leg and ankle.

My mind instantly thought, "Oh, Lord. One more thing against me, as well as the elements. Am I to die out here in the wilds? Am I to die out here without even knowing who I am?"

I thought about that considerably.

"No!" I thought, "I refuse to die! There is someone, somewhere, that I need to get to. I can feel her calling me."

Her? I closed my eyes and tried to remember the face. Once again it appeared and it nagged at the back of my mind—Who is this woman? Where is this woman? She just had to be somewhere South of here. I must keep going.

Painful as it was, I slowly put my sock and boot back on my swollen foot, gritting my teeth against the pain. I tried to rise but the pain was awful. I crumbled to my knees and sat there for long minutes.

The answer came to me. I needed a crutch of some kind. That would take a stout pole. I searched my surroundings. Being in the wilds, there was forest everywhere. I would get my crutch and be on my way once again.

Hours later found me hobbling along very slowly with a long pole that I had hacked off determinedly with the jackknife. I was glad that the blade was sharp.

I watched the sky carefully realizing that nightfall was near. I was cold, I was hungry, and I hurt all over. My head throbbed and I could feel sweat running down my chest. Even though feverish I had to go on. Just then, I stumbled and fell headfirst into the snow.

How long I lay there, I didn't know. It was dark when I opened my eyes, and again, I felt frozen to the core. Painfully, I reached out grabbing snow. Bringing it to my face, I rubbed it all over. Somehow, I was still alive, but why? I should have frozen to death.

❧   ❧   ❧

Laura Sumner was relentless in back tracking Warrior. It was slow going. In some cases, just as they had the trail, they lost it. They spread out and within long anxious minutes, found it again. Warrior had been running straight out and by the other tracks they found, had been set upon by not less than ten large wolves.

Still they continued. Until, finally, they came to another riverbank. Laura closed her eyes for a long moment.

"Oh, God. This is it. I can feel it."

The wranglers spread out and with ever watchful eyes searched the shoreline. It was Eli Johnson who saw it first. He couldn't believe his eyes.

"Miss Laura! I think that I've found something. Yes! I did. Look—right there in the sand, under the water. A Colt Revolver."

Eli dismounted to retrieve it. He reached into the icy cold water and lifted it. He brushed the mud off with his gloved hand. It was indeed a Colt .45 Revolver and on the walnut grip was carved the initials "RCS". Laura's newest wrangler, Luke Griffin, simply called "Griff" by the other boys, suddenly called out, "Hey! Here's a hat stuck in the brush along this boulder."

Griff dismounted to work it out of the entanglement. Laura rode up to him and looked down. He handed it up to her and watched her eyes as they widened a bit, and then she closed them. Tears flowed. Griff hung his head for a moment and looked away. Laura sat mesmerized on Mickey as she held the Stetson in her hands. It was Cole's.

Judd Ellison called out suddenly and all turned to look at him.

"All of you—quick, come here. Look at this! Those are some awful big cougar tracks. All right. Everyone look closer—all around. I want this area searched and read for tracks."

Every wrangler, along with Laura, dismounted and carefully looked around. They were astonished at what they found. This was **the place**. There were boot tracks, Warrior's tracks, and also those of a very large cougar.

The boys pieced it together. Cole Stockton had ridden around the high rock, when the cougar jumped. Cole had been driven from the saddle and lay in the mud while Warrior became the object of cougar interest. Warrior fought hard. They found that Cole was once back on his feet and staggering backward. And then, nothing but horse tracks—Warrior's tracks.

They each surmised the situation. Judd related it. "It appears that the cougar leaped at Cole. He lost his balance and both went into the river. He lost his hat and revolver right here at the same time. That was some powerful cat."

He continued, "We need to ride downstream on both sides of this river. We need to find where Cole or the cat came out."

Laura silently nodded her agreement. The Sumner Horse Ranch group mounted up. Juan Soccorro and Eli Johnson crossed the river against the extremely heavy current and once on the opposite side, Eli called back to the others.

"That there current is not safe for any but the strongest of swimmers. There is an unseen undertow and it is fierce."

Judd waved to them in acknowledgement then motioned them to work themselves downstream. An hour later they found the falls and marveled at it. It was steep and it was treacherous. One could imagine riding the rapids in a canoe to suddenly sail out over fifty feet and then to plunge downward to the rock formation below.

"My God! Look at that!" exclaimed Mike Wilkes.

Laura turned to face Judd. "I don't care about the falls, Judd. I feel that Cole is alive. Let's get down to the bottom and search around."

Judd replied, "All right, Laura. But, by the time we get down there, it will be dark. We'll make camp and check it in the morning."

"All right Judd. Please understand this, I have to know. One way or the other, I have to know for sure."

It was the next morning that they found the carcass of the cougar.

"God Almighty" remarked Eli, "That is a big cat—one of the biggest I ever seen or even heard tell of. Wait a minute—look there! This cat's been shot. Look! A bullet wound in its shoulder area. But, that ain't what killed it. Look at the way that it lays all mangled and such. No, it went over the falls fighting for its life."

Suddenly, Laura closed her eyes and announced loud enough for all to hear, "And so did Cole. I feel it. He went over the falls, the same as that cat. He was here—I feel it."

Judd looked at Laura. He could feel the pain in her heart.

"All right. We'll search both sides of the river from here down. We'll see if he crawled out or didn't."

An hour later, Juan called out, "I think I find something. It looks very much like a struggle in the mud."

He looked further.

"Something or someone crawl in the frozen grass here. Look below there. A large root growing from the embankment. Yes, maybe like someone grabbed onto that root and hold on. Then climb out here. There is somewhat of a trail—it goes that way." He pointed.

They followed the slight trail for over a hundred yards. Then it disappeared completely. A sudden, but violent blizzard had rushed through the area and covered what tracks that there were.

For several hours, the Sumner Horse Ranch group criss-crossed the area—a mile out and a mile wide. No tracks were found. Nothing. No trace of Cole Stockton or whoever or whatever seemingly made the imprints in the mud and subsequent snow. Judd turned solemnly to face Laura.

"Laura. As much as I hate to admit it. Cole is gone. Even if he did crawl out of that river, he was near frozen to death. He had no hat, no gun, no horse, and most likely no means to survive the below zero temperatures up here. If it were him that crawled out of the river, he would have been soaking wet and with the icy cold would have frozen to death somewhere. He may just be covered up with the snow and we can't find his body. It's no use now Laura. We have to turn back to the ranch. We are short on supplies and this is no place to be short on anything."

As much as Laura wanted to go on, she knew that Judd was right. After a long minute, she answered, "All right Judd. We'll turn back. But, in my mind, he is still alive. He is hurt and he needs help. I don't know why, but that image is still in my mind. Deep inside me, I feel a cry for help."

"I understand Laura. Laura—if there was at least some sign."

Judd swallowed hard, "Just some sign at all. We would follow it all the way. But, Laura—you see it. There is no sign. There is just no sign at all."

Tears flowed slowly down Laura's cheek as she nodded to Judd and softly said, "All right, Judd. Let's go home. Christmas Eve is only a day or so away. I want to be in my home for Christmas Day."

Judd nodded and gave the signal. All wranglers reluctantly turned to began the ride back to the Sumner Horse Ranch. All of the boys' thoughts turned to Laura. They loved this woman—this Boss Wrangler. She was their boss, but she was also their friend. What affected Laura affected each and every one of them. They would miss Cole Stockton just as she.

It was then that I felt their presence. I felt them before I heard the snarls and low growls. It was dark and they were hungering after my flesh. Suddenly, I could almost see their yellow eyes glowering at me from around thirty feet away. They just stood there, motionless, and wanting me.

I had just moved and they were a bit wary. It was the largest pack of timber wolves that I had ever seen in my time. Soon, they would get over their fear and rush me. But for now, they just stood and growled. It was a fearsome feeling.

That the pack would encircle me and come from all directions was clear in my mind. Why was that?

I reached to my side and drew the Colt. I opened the loading gate and withdrawing a single cartridge, from the belt, slipped it into the cylinder. I would need all that I could use, and in a hurry. I thought then to myself, "It's times like this that a man could use two revolvers."

It was like lightning struck me in the head. I had two revolvers. But where was the second one? I had no idea.

The wolves now began to spread out to ring me. I searched for the leader of the pack. I wanted to know him. The sound was crisp and clear as I cocked the Colt.

They circled warily. They had them a man—a hurt, sick, and starving man and they wanted him. They circled around and around, always watching for an opening.

I stood with my crutch and turned my head slowly with the leader while he circled. I looked for some ever so slight sign, as I figured that it would come from him first. Long minutes passed, and then, three large wolves dashed and leaped at the same time. I felt the Colt buck in my hand and all three jerked back with the impact of them .45's.

I watched more closely now as I carefully slipped out the expended brass. Reaching to my belt, I drew three more fresh cartridges and reloaded.

They came again and I was shooting. They were cunning and wily and some rushed in immediately for the kill that they just knew that they had. The Colt bucked in my hand and those wolves also lay crumpled and bleeding.

The wounded wolves were suddenly viciously attacked by the rest of the pack. They were literally torn limb from limb.

I took the occasion to shakily reload. This was a sight that somehow in the back of my mind I had been told of before by old timers of the West. It was bloody and it was pure death.

I quickly counted them now—there were close to a half dozen wolves with yellowish eyes and sharp fangs that drooled for flesh and blood and their taste was for me. With snarls and growls they all started at me at once. I fought for my life. The Colt bucked six times and more wolves jerked back with the impact. The others snarled in on me more warily.

With little chance to reload, I jerked that crutch up and almost fell to my knees. I steadied on my left foot and held that pole at the ready. The end was sharpened somewhat and I pointed it like a spear while I reached back to my cartridge belt and fumbled more bullets out. I counted six and slowly—still holding them at bay, turned the cylinder and one by one emptied the expended brass.

It was difficult in the freezing cold to load with one hand, holding the weapon close to my chest, but I done it, and watched them wolves too. Suddenly, they came at me again.

I impaled the first one with the "crutch pole" then, dropped it to swing the Colt and fire six times. More wolves died that round. The seemingly largest of the pack backed off for a moment and grew ever more violent in his growls and snarls.

I closed my eyes for only a moment as I reached to the cartridge belt and more bullets. There were none left. I grimaced with the realization. I had no more bullets and there was one wolf left and I thought, "Well, that's the law of nature. The strongest will survive."

I slipped my hand into the pocket of that heavy jacket and produced that jackknife. I holstered the Colt, it being useless now. I unfolded the knife and stood there waiting for that wolf.

As sick and exhausted as I felt, I was not going to give up and die. Something was calling me from the other side of the hills and I was going there to meet my destiny.

The wolf came straight at me. It leaped into the air and then the sudden weight hit me and knocked me down. I grappled with it, grabbing its throat and jabbing with that knife. It snarled into my face and I could smell the decayed breath as I continued to stab him again and again. Finally, I fell on top of him and holding on to his furry throat with all my strength, I plunged that knife as deep as I could into the lower throat and twisted the knife. Blood gushed everywhere. The animal suddenly let out an eerie gasp and then it was dead.

I rolled away from the carcass and lay there in the snow breathing hard. My head was pounding with pain. I wanted to close my eyes and sleep, but a voice suddenly entered my mind. A woman's voice. It was soft, warm, and directly jolted me.

"Cole."

I shuddered with the sound of that name. It had a distinctly familiar ring to it. I became more alert then and looked down at myself. My coat and clothing were torn almost to shreds. I felt the chill of the icy air and swallowed hard. I had to keep moving.

I could feel the chill of the sudden mountain blizzard coming in and coming fast. I knew somehow that within minutes I could be covered with snow and once again fighting for my life. I wondered if I had the strength for it. I wondered also if the good Lord had called my name and it was my time no matter what.

Had I cheated death so far? Just how close was it?

That blizzard streaked in on me just then, and I stumbled forward, clinging to my crutch and blinded by the flurries. I was freezing cold and I shivered with each painful step that I took. Still that voice was calling me and I just had to take another step.

At one point I fell again. I was so cold and numb that I almost wanted to just go to sleep and die right there. I would've too, had it not been for **that voice** once more calling me—"Cole." It rang in my ears and I forced myself up from the ground. I was in pain as I groped for my crutch and slowly pulled myself up on it. I forced myself forward again. I kept on and on—one foot in front of the other—always with the aid of my crutch. The voice got louder in my mind. "Cole Stockton."

"Huh? Somebody calling me?"

I looked around me and felt numb to the bone as the icy sleet sprayed my body. I looked to the sky. It was black and ominous. I once again moved step by step forward.

Suddenly a gradual hill formed in front of me. It looked to go up forever. I started up it. I was half way up to what seemed the top and I fell, face down. I was so numb from the cold that my legs and feet didn't want to move anymore. I lay there for a long minute breathing hard. Suddenly, that voice came to me again, "Cole Stockton, I love you."

I found myself moving. I was literally crawling up the hill, pulling myself by sheer will power. My legs were numb. I somehow reached the top of the hill and suddenly, I stared down at what seemed to be a ranch.

I mean that there were several buildings there. And all were lit up with lamps. I hung my head and cried.

I was weak with fever and frostbite. My legs didn't want to work—they were numb with cold. My clothes were shredded and sparse. I was bleeding from wounds and my head ached something fierce.

Still, I had to make it to the closest building. I at least had to make some sort of signal. I reached for the Colt at my side. I shook violently as I cocked it with both hands and squeezed off. A metallic *click*. I had no more bullets. I had to make it to those buildings on my own or die trying.

I moved slowly—always with those lamps in my eyes. I rolled myself down the hill and crawled some more. It was then that I looked up at the simple sign that read,

"Sumner Horse Ranch"

I cried tears that rolled down my cheeks and almost froze on my face. I crawled forward on my hands and knees, growing weaker by the moment.

The last one hundred feet to the steps of a white painted porch brought me to crawl on my stomach. My arms were tired and growing weaker, but I slowly pulled myself inch by inch to that porch. There were sounds coming from that house and I listened.

There was singing. There were people in that house and they were singing. They were singing some kind of Christmas songs.

I needed something to tell them that I was here. I needed desperately to tell them that I was here and needed help. I lowered my head to the porch step and lay there for a long moment.

"The Colt", I thought once again in feverish mind.

I shook as I drew it, cocked it, and squeezed the trigger. I was surprised as the hammer hit on cold metal and no other sound. It was only then that I remembered once again that I had no more bullets.

Still, if I could get their attention. I fumbled the Colt around in my hand and I tried to "hammer" with it. My fingers and hands were so cold that it was all I could do to just hold it in my hands. I had to get to the door of that house. Somehow, I had to get to the door.

I managed to slip the revolver back into the holster and then, with sheer determination, I crawled up them steps almost to the door. I lay there for a long moment. I was so cold. I was so froze, so hungry, so sick, and so numb that my body shivered with every move that I made. I hurt with so much pain. Still, I felt that I was within only minutes of being saved.

I painfully inched my way to the door and as I reached out my hand to tap at it, a voice rang loud and clear in my mind, "Cole Stockton, I love you with all my heart. You are alive and I will find you."

That voice again! The next words out of my mouth were "Laura. I am here. I need you."

My frozen fingers shook as I reached out and with heavily labored breath tried to tap on the door. I tried to move closer, but my body was so cold and weak that I could hardly move. Once again, I tried to tap at the door. I tried to yell out. My throat was dry. I hung my head and tried to think.

I gathered all the strength within me and tried again. I lightly tapped on the door with my fingers—I was reaching out for Laura.

❦   ❦   ❦

Laura Sumner and her wranglers were all gathered together in front of her Christmas tree. All held cups of strong black coffee, with a bit of old Irish whiskey to quell the cold.

They sang some traditional holiday songs and the boys presented Laura with their annual "gift". This year the boys had gotten Laura a special gift of a fine stud horse from a neighboring ranch. The boys had planned this one from early in the year and all chipped in to buy the service to a fine mare that Laura held in high esteem.

The boys kind of surrounded Laura and all looked at her closely. Judd Ellison summed it up. "Laura, we know how you felt about Cole. We want you to know that—well, iffen there was any chance at all, we would have ridden all the way to hell and back to find him for you."

Laura looked into each wrangler's eyes and softly said a simple, "Thank you. Thank you all for all you have done for me. I shall miss Cole very much. But if there would be only one Christmas gift that I could wish for and receive, it would be to just have him here with us right now."

At that moment, Lady, Laura's blonde haired dog, suddenly stood up from her mat in the corner and rushed up to Laura. Lady reached up and grabbed Laura's shirtsleeve in her mouth and would not let go. Lady seemed to be dragging Laura to the door.

Laura stopped in her tracks and held the dog to her side. She looked directly at the door to her home. She motioned for all to be still. There was an almost inaudible tapping.

Everyone listened hard and then, Laura walked with Lady to the door. Lady sniffed the door and then looked up into Laura's eyes. She barked loudly at Laura, and kept on barking.

Laura's face turned soft as she moved to the door. She turned her head and said, "God, please let it be."

Laura opened the door and looked down at the bloody, wretched looking, frozen figure laying just inches from her door.

"Oh my God! It's Cole! Help me with him. He is hurt and near frozen."

The Sumner Ranch family moved quickly. Cole Stockton was lifted and carried into the house as gently as possible. They laid him on the sofa in front of the fireplace and wrapped him in warm blankets. They spoon fed him hot tea laced with whiskey to warm his insides.

A pot of beef and vegetable stew was placed on the stove. He needed nourishment if he was to survive the night. His wounds were tenderly cared for.

Step by step, his friends labored to keep him alive.

Cole periodically shuddered in his sleep as if a wild northern wind had somehow grasped his soul and would not let go. Laura sat at his side throughout the night, tenderly speaking to him and placing warm cloths on his forehead. She continuously kept him covered with blankets because he kicked them off within throes of delirium.

One by one throughout the night, a wrangler sat with Laura and helped her, because she refused to leave Cole's side. Time and time again, Cole mumbled incoherent words. Sometimes, his right hand twitched a bit, then moved toward his waist clawing for something. He seemed more distressed with each clawing motion.

Eli Johnson just happened to be sitting with Laura. He saw Cole's motion and recognized it immediately. "Laura, he's a needing his gun—give it to him."

Laura reached to the foot of the bed where Cole's gunbelt hung. She slipped the Colt Revolver from the holster, flipped open the loading gate and ejected all six empty casings. She gently laid the butt of the pistol in his hand.

Immediately upon feeling the Colt in his hand, his fingers moved swiftly. They cocked the hammer back and squeezed the trigger in one fluid motion and then repeated it several times until with an audible sigh, Cole's right hand went limp and the revolver slipped from his hand to thud onto the floor.

Eli looked into Laura's widened eyes and remarked, "He's kilt whatever devil it was that he needed killing. I predict that he'll live."

And then, with a wide grin spreading on his whiskered face, Eli also remarked, "He's too dammed ornery to die."

Laura looked deeply into Eli's eyes and held them for a long moment. Suddenly, she smiled for the first time in several days. Yes, Cole Stockton was too dammed stubborn and just too dammed ornery to die. He had trekked on foot over thirty miles within extreme elements of danger until finally reaching her doorstep. She knew instinctively that he had survived snow, sleeting winds, and hunger. God, himself, knew what else Cole had survived in order to arrive on her doorstep at Christmas Eve.

She looked deeply into Eli's eyes and smiled. "Thank you, Eli. I'm alright now. You were right, but, I need to stay with him." Eli nodded affirmatively.

"Laura, I know how much you love him. We, all of us here at the ranch feel the same way. Cole is a part of all of us, and now, he's taught us another valuable lesson."

Laura looked into Eli's face and saw it aglow with understanding. She nodded. Cole had just taught them to never give up, even in the face of overwhelming odds, because HE was always there.

Later, within the small room that Cole Stockton occupied at the Sumner Ranch, Laura knelt beside the bed and looked upon the wretched sleeping figure that had suddenly appeared at her door on Christmas Eve. With soft tears of love in her eyes and renewed faith, she whispered,

"Thank you Lord. You have given me the most wonderful gift of all—the gift of life for someone that I dearly love."

978-0-595-40003-4
0-595-40003-5